"SO, JERMAINE, CAN I ASSUME THAT IF YOU FOUND A WOMAN YOU COULD CONNECT WITH ON EVERY LEVEL, YOU'D MARRY HER?" CANDACE ASKED.

Jermaine appeared surprised by the question. "Why *wouldn't* I?"

"Because some brothers are scared to commit, even if they have found someone who fulfills them on every level. Putting myself in the shoes of your fans, I'm just curious to know what you would do."

"I'm not afraid of commitment. And I think a love like that is a beautiful thing." He began laughing nervously. "Yeah, I'd marry her."

"The great Jermaine Hill, the golden-voiced speaker who inspires the country about life and all—I didn't think I'd ever get to see you nervous."

"I'm not nervous," he quickly retorted.

"Oh, really?"

"Really."

They walked along silently for another quarter mile or so. Candace silently relished her interview success. She had finally broken through that macho wall of his to witness his genuine emotion. Arguably, it was the first honest emotion he had displayed so far this week . . .

a MAN INSPIRED

Derek Jackson

Walk Worthy Press

West Bloomfield, Michigan

WARNER BOOKS

NEW YORK BOSTON

The events and characters in this book are fictitious. Certain real locations and public figures are mentioned, but all other characters and events described in the book are totally imaginary.

Published by Warner Books with Walk Worthy Press™

Warner Books

Time Warner Book Group
1271 Avenue of the Americas, New York, NY 10020

Walk Worthy Press
33290 West Fourteen Mile Road #482, West Bloomfield, MI 48322

Visit our Web sites at www.twbookmark.com and www.walkworthypress.net.

Printed in the United States of America

First Edition: January 2005
10 9 8 7 6 5 4 3 2 1

Library of Congress Cataloging-in-Publication Data

Jackson, Derek.
A man inspired / Derek Jackson.
p. cm.
ISBN 0-446-69352-9
1. Motivational speakers—Fiction. 2. Self-help techniques—Fiction.
3. Depression, Mental—Fiction. 4. Suicidal behavior—Fiction. I. Title.
PS3610.A348M36 2005
813'.6—dc22
2004009582

Book design and text composition by L&G McRee

For Mom and Dad,
you two are truly my inspirations.

acknowledgments

First of all, to my Lord and Savior, Jesus Christ, for blessing me with the opportunity and time to do what I love—the glory is all Yours.

To my parents, Doris and Nokomis Jackson Jr., thank you for supporting and encouraging me in every way possible.

Denise Stinson—thank you for believing in me and providing the avenue to get this work published. The vision of Walk Worthy Press is so needed today—you're a beacon of light!

To Marina Woods, for your encouragement and for introducing me to Denise—what can I say? A million thanks.

Dr. Courtney Walker, your constant encouragement and living example mean so much to my life. You are a true friend.

To Bishop Shelton Bady and Sister Kim Bady, thank you for always being examples of excellence and godliness.

To Bishop T. D. Jakes—your ministry continually motivates me to reach for the highest heights.

To the knowledgeable, friendly people at Warner Books and in particular the wonderful editorial skills of Frances Jalet-Miller—thank you.

To the authors who have encouraged me—Brandilyn Collins, Maurice Gray Jr., Ruth Mayfield, Brad Meltzer—many, many thanks!

To Frank Peretti and Ted Dekker—you both continue to blaze a literary trail I hope to follow.

To the Jackson and May families and the employees of Anadarko Petroleum in The Woodlands, Texas—your encouragement has sustained me along the journey. Thank you!

a MAN INSPIRED

prologue

THE OLD WOMAN knelt at the foot of the bed, rocking slowly back and forth on aching, swollen knees as she voiced aloud her heartfelt prayer to God. The simple act of praying had always come easily to her, a blessing at the moment because unfortunately her once-vibrant memory was deteriorating fast. Her doctors had diagnosed her with Alzheimer's disease several years previously, but Bell Davis wasn't about to let that negative report prevent her from having daily lil' talks with Jesus. With withered hands, she resolutely clutched a six-inch-long golden cross that had faithfully been handed down through five generations from her ancestry as she focused her heart, soul, and breath for the task of intercession. Her prayer today, like each day the past few months, was targeted toward the one problem currently sticking in her side like the proverbial thorn.

Twenty-eight years ago she had taken in and then begun raising her sister Shirley's three-year-old child, Jermaine. Bell hadn't been exactly thrilled to do such a thing but she didn't have a choice, really. Both Shirley and her husband had been addicts—hopelessly strung out on crack cocaine that rendered them completely unfit and unable to take care of their only child. So rather than see the young boy become a ward of the state, Bell rescued him from that drug-infested home and brought him to live with her in Baltimore, where she could raise him in an atmosphere filled with love and hope. He had been a mischievous little kid, but what was the saying everybody always observed with knowing smirks on their faces? *Boys will be boys . . .*

As he continued to grow and develop into a man, Bell noticed that he was anything but an ordinary young boy. In fact, for Bell he was truly a little gift from God. Jermaine possessed a unique ability to speak publicly in a way that commanded the attention of anyone listening. With rich, melodious tones, his vocal style, cadence, and flair naturally conjured up images of the most powerful of public speakers—and accordingly, that was the life he had chosen to lead. After securing a four-year, all-expenses-paid scholarship to Howard University, he had graduated a year early as a media communications major with his sights set on making a name for himself.

And he certainly had done *just* that. Now grown and living on his own in the glitzy, star-studded lights of Hollywood, Jermaine appeared to have realized his childhood dream. As the key figure in a successful motivational-speaking business, he was now generally recognized as the foremost inspirational guru in the country. And like any mother, Bell had been so very proud to see Jermaine achieve such a staggering level of success. Still, despite the seemingly wonderful glamour and riches that the world was lavishly heaping upon him, Bell knew there was something still not quite right in her baby's heart. A night didn't go by when she didn't have the same terrible, haunting dreams concerning him. Dreams that revealed what she knew was taking place in those dark, secret closets of his life.

"Save my son, oh God . . ." she cried out hoarsely between broken sobs. The past few weeks she had so poured out her soul that there were no more tears left to shed. All she had now were broken, choppy heaves of exhausted, worn-out lungs. "S-s-save . . . my . . . so-oo-oon!" The indescribable anguish now piercing her heart was a pain only a mother could intimately know and suffer. Though she had not actually given birth to Jermaine, she had raised that young man like he was her very own. So it didn't matter what anyone else said—Jermaine Hill was . . . her *son*.

"Save my son . . . breathe life into him, oh, God . . . breathe life into him . . ." She knew that Jermaine couldn't hear her. But that wasn't the important thing. She knew her Heavenly Father was listening.

• • •

NO LESS THAN THE WORLD had been offered to him, and every fiber of his being should have been reveling in such incredible favor and opportunity. It was certainly well within his right to do such a thing—most men would have sacrificed much to experience the height of fame and recognition that was now being afforded to him. But this Saturday morning found Jermaine nervously spinning the compact black Colt .22

pistol around on palms and fingers clammy with perspiration. In his mind he replayed a half-dozen or so scenarios, none of which were pleasant and all of which involved the one bullet chambered in the pistol being fired in the direction of his head. Though this was his first try at Russian roulette, the game's gruesome twists of chance were not applicable to him, really. Because who needed the distraction of probability when for some godforsaken reason you actually wanted to kill yourself?

In reality, he should have been the last person in this predicament. Twenty-four months was all the time it had taken for him to climb to the top of virtually every nationally recognized list along the motivational speaker's circuit. A month from now and he would have his own cable show to supplement the wildly popular one-hour segment he currently did for national radio. Wildly popular, indeed. Not only were calls from the late night network interview shows pouring in daily, but he also was courting several publishers for a book deal that would reportedly be the largest ever offered to a motivational speaker.

Not that any of that mattered to Jermaine right now. From where he sat on his bed, he lifted his tired eyes and allowed his gaze to linger forlornly on the framed pictures of Ronny and Eric resting atop his tempered glass nightstand. His two best friends from his undergrad days at Howard University, they had been killed in a car accident on this very day nine years earlier. To tell the truth, they had been closer than friends to him; they had become the brothers he had never known in the loneliness of a solitary childhood experience. But they were gone now, and their tragic deaths had triggered Jermaine's catastrophic relapse into a fragile, private shell of an existence with no outlet for his feelings. The loss of true friendship and brotherhood for him was almost unbearable, even after almost a decade had gone by, for he had painfully learned that when you're famous, nobody wants to be with you for the *person* you are inside. The sad truth was that nobody really cared about the *person* you were—the only thing that mattered was the rapid accumulation of money, fame, and prestige. People entered and exited his life in a much-trafficked revolving door, with every new person inevitably bringing ulterior motives for gaining access to his inner circle. After a while, he discovered that the only person he could really trust was himself, which in turn became a problem once he began to forget just who he himself was.

Lifting the gun to his head with shaking hands, Jermaine pressed it firmly between his eyes. The barrel was starkly cool against his fevered skin. He wanted to cry but there were no more tears left for him to shed. This from a man whose smooth baritone voice was heard on the airwaves all over the country. By the past year, at the age of thirty, he had traveled to every continent in the world. There was enough money in his bank accounts to finance a who's-who of A-list parties every weekend. To willingly share his bed, he'd had the kind of women who typically graced the cover of beauty magazines. He'd driven exclusive, custom-made cars that could not even be purchased from the average automobile dealerships.

This was Jermaine Hill, whom the country had

fallen in love with in two short years. The man with the golden voice who was fast becoming an icon in urban lore. A star of stars. A celebrity of celebrities.

But on this Saturday morning, sitting alone in his room at a quarter past nine, Jermaine Hill had a gun to his head. And he was playing a dangerous game at which he was hoping to succeed.

PART I

Character is what you are. Reputation is what you make people believe you are.

—ANONYMOUS

chapter one

CANDI, CANDI, TURN YOUR radio on, girlfriend! My show is about to come on, and you know how gooo-ood that man makes me feel." Candace simply rolled her eyes as her fingers continued their rapid, fluttery dance atop her laptop's keyboard. She was fifty words from finishing her last paragraph for the *Ebony* magazine column, and not even her best friend, Tasha, was going to cause her to lose focus just now.

"Candi, you hear what I just said?"

Candace nodded twice as she continued staring at the computer screen with steely brown eyes that refused to blink. Twenty words. Her last sentence.

"Candi, you're gonna make me hurt you . . . I'm not playing . . . I—"

"Taa-daa!" came the writer's exclamation, purposely cutting off her friend's voice. She pressed the key command to save her article, then fashioned a graceful pose with her fingers outstretched like a gymnast who has just vaulted into the air, flipped multiple times, and landed without stumbling. A perfect ten.

"Are we done now, Dear Miss Black Abby? Because

if you make me miss Jermaine Hill, trust me—it ain't gon' be a pretty sight."

Candace reluctantly lowered her hands and somehow suppressed a desire to throw one of her pillows at Tasha. Her thinking was that if it hit Tasha's head, it would certainly do more good than damage.

"Black Abby, huh? Now that's original. Did you take all morning to think of that, or did it just come to you?"

"As a matter of fact, I was up half the night thinking about it," Tasha responded with a smile as she leaped off the bed and dashed over to the stereo. Within seconds the announcer's intro to the program she and millions of others loved and listened to entered the spacious bedroom in surround sound.

"Everybody in America, listen up! It's time for the hottest hour on the radio waves! If you're driving your car, get over to the slow lane; if you're at work, then take a lunch break and turn the volume way, way up! 'Cause coming to you right now is the most dynamic speaker in the nation today, the man with the golden voice guaranteed to get you excited and inspired about life! Here he is, America—Jermaaaaaaiiiiinnnnne Hiiiiiiilllllll!"

The pulsating beat and feel-good lyrics of Kool & the Gang's "Celebration," the standard music accompanying Jermaine Hill's intro, rang out all over the room.

As Candace re-fluffed the five lace embroidered pillows now strewn all over her bedspread from Tasha's hasty departure, she laughed out loud at her friend's pitiful attempts to dance in tune with the popular song.

"Shhh, Candi! He's about to come on!"

"This is Jermaine Hill once again coming to you live with an OD of inspiration for your soul," proclaimed the smooth, sexy voice through the speakers. "That's right—an overdose, because you and I both know you need it. So let's kick things off with my theme for today—how to make every day meaningful."

"Oh Jermaine, yeeesss," cooed Tasha. "Help me to make my days more meaningful!"

Candace caught Tasha's eye and made a brief gagging motion with her hands at her throat. "I can't believe I'm letting this go on in my own bedroom," she mumbled. "What is it with you and this guy, anyway? His material isn't *that* good."

"Shh!!!" Tasha's fiery glare made it clear that Candace was treading on some very thin ice.

Fine, Tasha, fine . . . Never mind that this is my house you're flappin' those lips in. And my own bedroom for that matter . . .

Jermaine Hill continued speaking. "Don't you sometimes wonder where all the time goes? Those days turn into weeks, months, and before you know it another year has gone by. And what do you have to show for it? More debt? More family problems? More promises you made to yourself that have gone unresolved? Yeah, you're going around in circles, aren't you? A cycle that leaves you distracted, unfulfilled, and wanting more." He paused for a second.

"So how do we change that, hmm? How can we make our days more meaningful? Let Jermaine give you some simple suggestions . . ."

• • •

CANDACE SLIPPED OUT OF her bedroom a few moments later, leaving Tasha all alone with her radio fantasy man, and made her way down the spiral staircase, shaking her head at her friend's naïveté. Then again, if listening to Jermaine Hill inspired Tasha, who was Candace to say otherwise?

That poor girl is going to do what she wants . . . that'll never change . . . I still love ya, though . . .

Opening the custom-made ivory French doors that led into her sunroom, she stepped gracefully across the threshold and inhaled deeply. The intermingling smells of the richly polished golden oak floor, the white gardenia–scented potpourri baskets on the bar countertop, and the French vanilla candles lit on the coffee table immediately filled Candace's senses. Of the five bedrooms, four bathrooms, den, kitchen, and dining room that were enclosed in the spacious house, this room was definitely her favorite. There was a uniquely feminine atmosphere saturating the room, from the soft and sensual fragrances to the lavender and gold pillows embellishing the cream-colored sofa to the paintings hanging along the walls. The three large canvas prints adorning the room were intimate portraits depicting various stages of womanhood—a young girl playing hopscotch, a mother nursing an infant child at her breast, and a grandmother looking to the heavens clutching a worn Bible to her bosom.

Incidentally, this was the only room in the house where she did not (and in fact, could not) write anything at all. No magazine columns, articles, poetry, or short stories were birthed in here; no, there wasn't so much as a sheet of paper or a pen in the entire room. This was her getaway—a personal refuge and sanctuary where she could fully celebrate being a woman—and where she could taste the savory fruits of success that life had bestowed upon her.

Three years ago at the ripe old age of twenty-six, she had become a syndicated columnist for a nationally distributed magazine; at twenty-eight her published collection of feature stories had reached the "you've made it now" status of the top ten on the *New York Times* best-seller list; and last year, she had been considered for a Pulitzer Prize after capturing the moving story of a Dallas schoolteacher's fight to be reinstated after being fired when her district found out that she was HIV-positive. Though Candace hadn't won the Pulitzer for that feature, the young columnist was nevertheless making waves in the journalism industry as a voice to be seriously reckoned with. It didn't matter that she had what was usually considered to be two strikes against her—being both a minority and a woman—because whenever *Candace Clark* was written on the byline, chances were very good that it was a story worth reading.

She leisurely strolled over to the large bay window next to the bar and gazed outside. It was late April in Houston, and the brightness of the shining sun's reflection cast shimmering ripples across the top of the water in her backyard pool. Not that she herself swam—the pool was just another fruit of her success—but such amenities would come in handy at times; for example, in a few weeks she would be hosting a reception at her home.

"I've become just like my mother in that way," she told herself, thinking again of how her late mother, Analee Clark, used to sit her down in a chair when she was a little girl to teach her how to be a prim and proper lady at dinner parties. Taught her how, on the night before a gala, to sleep in such a way so as to not mess up the expensive perm in her hair, how to sit with her legs demurely crossed at the ankles, how to wait for others to begin dining before you started eating, which fork and spoon to use, and so on. Somehow Analee had known that her daughter would grow up into a beautiful lady and continue the legacy of the Clark debutante tradition. And so, partly to honor the memory of her mother, Candace would from time to time hold lavish engagements at her home—NAACP fund-raisers, benefits for the Ensemble Theatre, the Urban League, NABJ. Mostly, though, she hosted the extravagant parties because they were wonderful opportunities to network and stay abreast of cultural happenings around the country. She could gather more information for features from just one of her parties than through days of sifting through the latest reports from the AP wire. It never ceased to amaze her how much people loved to dish when you wined and dined them.

Just below the bar's counter was a beehive-shaped cluster of bottle racks that held only nonalcoholic beverages. Her choice of beverages was deliberate; when she was growing up, she had one too many uncles who excessively indulged in alcohol. One haunting memory from her adolescence was of an uncle's trying to force himself on her in a drunken stupor. Ever since that day merely the smell of alcohol justifiably repulsed her.

Now, she retrieved a sparkling apple cider, removed the cork from the bottle, and half filled a tumbler that was already on the counter. To her surprise, all the fond recollections of her mother had caused tears to well up at the corners of her eyes. She quickly dabbed them away.

God, it seems like just yesterday . . .

"Here's to you, Analee," she whispered, raising the glass. Her mind's eye could vividly see the petite, lithe woman who had poured so much love and knowledge into her life. "Here's to everything that you've given me." It was a fitting, commemorative toast to a touching occasion, and as Candace took a sip of the bubbling drink she couldn't help but notice the twinge of sadness that was tugging at her heart. It would be six years to the day next Thursday that Analee had lost her valiant battle with breast cancer.

"Get it together, Candi," she encouragingly and firmly said to herself after drinking the last drops of cider from the tumbler. "Tasha's the emotional basket case, not me."

• • •

"THAT'S ALL THE TIME I have, people," Jermaine announced as he prepared the send-off to the broadcast. "So until we talk again, remember to be good to yourself, work hard before you play hard, treat your mama right, and if you can't say something nice . . ."

At this moment, he pressed the button for the recording of what could only be described as a ghetto-fied, high-pitched squeal of a voice (an animated Chris Tucker, perhaps) shouting, *"then keep your mouth shut!"*

Taking off his headset, he swiveled around in his chair and confidently strolled to the door of KKTL's recording studio. The station manager, Vic Trevino, was waiting in the hallway with a high five for his star host.

"You're on top of the game as always, my man! Muy bien, muy bien. Our numbers for the last quarter were off the charts again—the best ratings in Orange County!" The short, fiery Hispanic man shook his head then, wagging his finger and playfully giving Jermaine the kind of look a school principal ordinarily would give a tardy student. "I'm warning you, though. You keep this kind of behavior up and you're going to force me to restructure our entire budget just to keep you on the payroll."

"Hey Vic—you just do what you need to do," Jermaine countered as he flashed his trademark winning smile. "Because I'm gonna handle my business, you can best believe that."

Vic laughed quickly. A little too quickly, almost. "Oh I believe that, my man. I certainly do." The manager stole a glance over his shoulder, a little guiltily, then inched closer to Jermaine. "In fact, since I know how well you're gonna handle your business, I gotta little something for you," he said, lowering his voice, not that there was a need to, since they were the only ones in the hallway. Jermaine arched an eyebrow slightly—otherwise his face was a blank slate. Favors offered to him under-the-table and special unsolicited treatment were nothing new anymore. His growing clout was making him A-list; just last week he had strolled into Spago Beverly Hills without a reservation, yet still managed to be seated in the finest booth in the restaurant.

Vic produced two tickets from his inside coat pocket and handed them to Jermaine. "These are for the Lakers' play-off game this Sunday, my friend."

Jermaine barely even looked at the purple-and-gold-trimmed pieces of paper. "I already got tickets, Vic."

"Yeah?" The manager didn't even blink, didn't miss a beat. "But did I mention *where* these seats are located? Courtside, amigo. Right behind Jack Nicholson himself."

Jermaine turned to Vic with a wide smile. "Now *that's* what I'm talking about." He delicately lifted the tickets from Vic's hand like they were precious, rare, imported diamonds. "And this is my reward for simply taking care of business?"

"That's right." He approvingly held out his hands in the manner of a proud *padre.* "That's all I'm asking for, my friend."

Jermaine, of course, knew better than that. By now it was commonly known throughout the industry that his own agent was fielding offers from various radio and television studios since his two-year contract with KKTL was set to expire in December. Vic had more than enough reason to be worried about losing his most visible employee to these tempting opportunities, so in hopes of re-signing his star he had been handling Jermaine with royal treatment from the year's onset.

"Muchas gracias, Vic."

"Aha!" The proud *padre* became even prouder. "So you *have* been listening to that easy-learning Spanish tape I gave you, hmm?"

"Yeah, but I'm only using it for the parts that let me rap to those fine Latino mamas in East L.A."

They both shared a good laugh over that one, although as Jermaine moved on down the hallway, he thought Vic's facial expression still seemed a bit strained.

• • •

THE SNARLED TRAFFIC ON Interstate 5 forced Jermaine's onyx-black Cadillac Escalade into an insulting crawl as he traveled away from downtown Los Angeles, heading north to a studio address in Burbank. According to his agent, he was scheduled to do a taped interview for some late-night television show, but that certainly didn't mean that he was in a big rush. Not only was he unsure as to which show it was; he honestly didn't care, either. It was all becoming one big continual bore to him, this unending life under a microscope of celebrity. Host a benefit dinner here, attend a movie premiere there, shake a few hands back over there again and please, Mr. Hill, don't forget to smile for the camera right here.

The people pulling on his time and skyrocketing fame had no clue as to who he really was. If you read the *New Yorker,* then you knew Jermaine Hill to be the larger-than-life motivational guru with the golden voice and requisite sex appeal to be a bona fide star.

Vibe described him as having the political savvy of Tavis Smiley delivered with a Master P hip-hop blend. And word on the street had it that he was slated to be on the cover of the next issue of *Ebony* magazine.

"All this fame," he ruefully thought to himself. *"And don't nobody have a clue . . ."*

The ring of his cell phone interrupted the tap-tap-tap of his fingers drumming on the soft leather of the steering wheel. In this bumper-to-bumper traffic, he had been monitoring how quickly the Escalade's gas gauge was plummeting toward empty. He swore the thing was the equivalent of an automotive black hole when it came to gas mileage, but it was all about keeping up appearances now. It wouldn't do for him to still be rolling in that '92 Toyota he had been driving when he was first hired on at KKTL.

"Jermaine Hill. Speak to me."

"J! Where you at, man?" It was his do-everything agent, Mario Jordan—better known as Super Mario to the industry people who over the years had observed the merciless manner in which he brokered deals and negotiated contracts. "You've got the brass at NBC sweatin' through those buttonhole suits, wondering where you are. The taping starts in sixty!"

"Mario, my bad, man, but I'm not going anywhere right now. Traffic on the Golden State is backed up for days."

"You're on the Golden State?" Mario cursed. "Reports say there's an eighteen-wheeler overturned just after Ventura."

"That explains why this road looks like the parking lot at the Rose Bowl with all these jammed cars. Hey listen, let's just cancel and do the show later." That was really what he wanted to do anyway. He was sick of all these celebrity obligations.

"No, J, we can't do that. They've been running promo spots for this for two weeks. We'll be blacklisted if we back out now. Wait a minute, wait a minute. Just thought of something. Are you close to Colorado?"

"Yeah. I'm just past Griffith Park. That's the next exit."

"Okay, okay. This might work, this might work. Listen, take Colorado, hang a right, and park in that empty lot next to the Best Western. I'll take care of everything from there."

"Whaddya mean, you'll take care of everything from there? I'm telling you, there's no way I can make it on time."

"Now *there's* where you're wrong, J. Hey, they don't call me Super Mario for nothing—don't forget that I'm worth every penny that comes my way."

Yeah . . . and most of them pennies be comin' out of my pocket . . . "Alright, fine. But don't keep me in the dark on this. What happens after that? What's the big plan?"

Mario confidently laughed. It was the knowing and shrewd sound of a man with more tricks up his sleeve than Houdini. "Just watch for the helicopter, J. I've got a friend of mine from LAX flying in to pick you up as we speak."

"Ah, friends," Jermaine mockingly thought as he clicked off his cell phone. It was almost laughable how they had a way of coming out of the woodwork when you were the current flavor of the month.

chapter two

THE INCREASING NUMBER of African-American press imprints popping up around the country and the rise of e-commerce as a legitimate consumer option all had spelled out *golden opportunity* for Myra Washington. Because by her fortieth birthday, she had made the frightening discovery that there really was a glass ceiling preventing her from rising any higher in corporate America. Frightening indeed, because she certainly had not gone to Spelman College in Atlanta, majored in speech communication, and graduated with honors just to type letters and fetch coffee all day. Especially for some backwater company that could care less about who she was as an individual or what she had to offer them.

So after a life-changing weekend attending one of T. D. Jakes's mega *Woman Thou Art Loosed!* conferences at the Georgia Dome, she had been motivated to stir up the faith lying dormant inside her and pursue a dream that had first taken root while she was co-editing *The Messenger*, Spelman's alumnae publication, during her senior year. That had been back in the 1980s, when the chances of a black woman making significant strides in the white-collar world of journalism were as realistic as a fly not being noticed in a tray of buttermilk. Yes, Myra had the door-opening powers of a college degree and she by no means lacked ambition or determination, but she also had . . . a baby boy. Tyrone Jr. The first Tyrone, that fast-talking, fine-looking brother she had met during her sophomore year, had swept her off her feet with his promises to "show her a good time" while in college. Well, who was she in 1978 to know the conniving ways of college men? Who was she but a country girl from Macon whose previous experience of a "good time" was an awkward, hurried French kiss on her prom night in the back of her uncle's barn? Good time, her behind.

So, saddled with little Tyrone Jr., upon graduation she was faced with the daunting prospect of not only landing a job, but also landing one quickly at that. After a few weeks, she had managed to find an administrative position that, while having no relevance to her communications degree, at least paid the bills. As the years passed, though, the lightbulb illuminating her college dream had depressingly waxed dimmer and dimmer.

Eighteen long, patience-building years later she was freed at last, financially speaking. Her little baby Tyrone had grown up, graduated from high school, and was now on his way to Quantico, Virginia, to begin a career in the Marine Corps. She would worry about him even more now that he was in the armed forces, but that automatically came with the job description of being a mother. She imagined that she would fret over her baby boy until the day she died. However, the Marines were taking care of Tyrone now, so the little extra money she had saved could finally be put to use pursuing her dream of running her very own magazine.

And so pursue she had. *Song of Solomon* had been launched in the summer of 2001 and while the unique name alone attracted many curious readers, the success of the magazine's format—blending spiritual themes with current societal issues—helped to retain those same readers. Now just three years into publication, Myra felt that all her magazine lacked was that one big, groundbreaking story to take it to the forefront of the urban market share. And with the phone call she had just received this late April afternoon, she was beginning to see a *golden opportunity* all over again.

"Xavier, are you sure your info is correct?" Her voice, suddenly breathless, was full of nervous anticipation as she spoke over the phone to her West Coast features reporter, Xavier Rollins. He was not only the magazine's prayer intercessor, but he was equally adept at digging up noteworthy background material for the magazine.

"Myra, I'm positive. This is coming straight from Mario Jordan's own mouth. He says the exclusive to publish the feature is open to any magazine, with one exception—Mario has the final choice on the writer."

For months now, the nation's top magazines had been in an intense bidding war, behind closed doors and off the record, over the rights to an all-access interview with Jermaine Hill. This meant the chance to go everywhere the star speaker went—documenting all his public appearances and in effect becoming his personal, journalistic shadow for two weeks.

"Whomever Mario wants to write it doesn't matter!

We're prepared to spare no expenses over the chance to land this one—this is going to be the biggest interview of the year!"

"The guy knows that. That's why he's letting it be known that whoever ultimately lands this story will be the one who can also land Candace Clark."

"But . . . but that's *Ebony*'s girl!" Myra exclaimed as she started to get a sickening feeling in the pit of her stomach. "She does that column for them and everything."

"Yeah, she writes for them, but technically she's not under contract when it comes to interviews like this. She's a freelancer, and from what I've been hearing, she's been looking to expand her options."

"How so?"

"Well, my sources tell me—"

"Oh, here we go again with you and your sources!"

Xavier laughed. "This is how the game is played, Myra. Remember? Anyway, my sources are telling me that she likes to take a chance every now and then, if the opportunity is right."

"If the opportunity is right? This story is not even close to being a *chance*. It's the single biggest scoop of the year. Why would an accomplished writer like her leave the comfort zone of the big-names and write this under *Song of Solomon*?"

"Listen to this—I have very good information that from time to time she likes to write for the lesser-known, independent magazines. I guess it appeals to her in some way. She's gotten her fame from her best-selling book and all, but it's not a coincidence that the column that got her nominated for the Pulitzer was written in a small Dallas medical journal."

"So what are you saying?"

"I'm saying that she's not a lock to write this story for the big-names like you're automatically assuming. And not only that, I think if you go to Houston and personally talk to her, you just may be surprised with what you find out."

• • •

THE SOFT, STIRRING SOUNDS coming faintly from the young woman lying next to him meant that she hadn't fallen asleep just yet. And Jermaine was going to make sure that she didn't, either. To him, there was nothing worse than having to make small talk in the morning and pretend that what had just happened was anything more than a one-night stand.

He roughly nudged her bare shoulder with his hand, causing a sleepy moan to come from her. He had met the woman, who said she was an actress (weren't they all?), while at a party in North Hollywood earlier that day. After the third round of drinks, one thing had led to another and the next thing both of them knew, they were in bed together. For her, sleeping with the one and only Jermaine Hill was probably something she'd proudly retell with a warped sense of pride to all her girlfriends; for him, it had been just another way to pass the evening.

"Hey, baby, you up?" He vaguely remembered her name started with a D, but he had forgotten what. Or more likely, he had never asked in the first place.

"Mmm . . . yeah. Where's my clothes?"

"Think you left them in the bathroom."

"Okay. Mmm . . . yeah, that's right. Thanks, Jermaine. Oh honey, you were . . . awesome."

Jermaine rolled his eyes and turned on his back as the girl slowly and somewhat dreamily made her way to the bathroom. She turned on the light and closed the door.

He got up seconds later, stretched, and strolled to his balcony patio overlooking the vast, scenic Hollywood Hills. The small one-bedroom condominium was not much for size, but the enviable location made it the perfect bachelor pad for just about any guy in the world looking to have a good time whenever he wanted. Tonight, the ivory- and golden-hued moon high above the Pacific Southwest was just a half-crescent, though it still reflected enough light to brilliantly illuminate the rolling hills and coarse terrain of the valley. And it was at that moment, leaning against the wooden railing of his deck, that Jermaine was once again left to wonder what in the world he was doing wrong.

What am I missing? Don't I have it all? People would kill to be me . . . and I would kill . . . to stop being me . . . The thought was so unbelievably ironic that he would have laughed out loud if it hadn't also been so frighteningly close to the truth.

When he was a kid, his Aunt Bell had tended to be overprotective about which influences he was exposed to, in effect limiting his life to a strict circle of school, church, and some occasional sporting events. But talk about your reverse effects—all *that* had succeeded in doing was to create an overpowering thirst in his mind to truly see the world—a thirst to catch up on everything he missed while being raised under the iron grip of stringent religious doctrine, to experience all the thrills he could now squeeze out of the rest of his life. So he craved the fame. Sought the money. Romanced the girls. And by all accounts, he had been successful in all three categories.

So why . . . am I still . . . not happy?

"Jermaine?" D-whatever-her-name-was stepped out onto the balcony, clad now in the flimsy, red cocktail dress she had been wearing when they first met. "Honey, are you sure you don't want me to stay longer? I don't mind spending the night."

"No, I got some things I need to do," he replied tersely, not even bothering to look back at her.

She came up close behind him and touched him on the shoulder. "Well, alright then. Until next time . . ."

Jermaine was sure there wouldn't be a next time, but there wasn't any point in telling her.

• • •

AN HOUR LATER, as he slowly cruised down Sunset Boulevard with his tinted windows all the way up, the plan slithered its way into his mind again. It had never really wandered from his thoughts in the first place after disguising itself as a harmless little idea at Ronny and Eric's funeral almost a decade ago. And given that many years to develop and fester, it now was an uncontrollable raging monster of suicidal tendencies. Through the distorted eyes of blinding grief, he had viewed his two friends as being in a place where there was no more hurt. No more pain. They had gone and left him behind all alone in this world, and for some reason, it had been an extremely appealing notion if he were to somehow join them.

They say only crazy people contemplate suicide . . .

If all the millions of people that listened to his show knew what he was contemplating at the moment, they would probably renounce him as a star motivational guru, or whatever it was they had dubbed him.

That's right, America. Call me crazy. Stark, raving, time-for-the-straitjacket crazy . . .

Glancing at the speedometer on the Escalade, he wondered how fast he could push the expensive SUV if he were on an open road—one of those hilly, curvy California freeways that skirted the Pacific Ocean. That had become the new plan, because the idea involving the .22 was just too grisly. And too messy. Driving off a cliff at a hundred and twenty miles an hour sounded much easier, if indeed such things could be termed *easy.*

He pulled off to the side of the road and turned down the volume on the radio, not caring to be entertained anymore by music. At the moment, the radio stations in Orange County weren't satisfying his musical tastes, anyway. He had been a large collector and lover of jazz back in college, from the greats like Dizzy, Thelonius Monk, and Louis Armstrong to Charlie Parker, Count Basie, George Benson, and the early Quincy Jones. Back then, life had seemed simpler, truer, freer. To be completely surrounded by great thinkers and creative geniuses at that time in his young adult life had been water to his thirsty soul. At no time before or since had he been around so many black folk who challenged him to excel in both the classroom and life.

Two in particular, Ronny Mayfield and Eric Swann, he had met at a Greek party on campus during his freshman year. All of them had grown up in the D.C. area, Ronny from the Lafayette Courts in Baltimore and Eric from the Edgewood Terrace housing projects in D.C. Jermaine himself had originally been born in Brooklyn, but had been raised by his Aunt Bell in Baltimore from the age of three when his own crack-addicted parents couldn't stay clean long enough to care for him.

Ronny and Eric became the brothers he never had as an only child who had been reared by his old aunt. An aunt who, although she loved him dearly, couldn't relate to him as a growing man. The trio had become inseparable during their four years at Howard, bonding like few men did anymore in modern society. Eric had been a political science major who had plans to graduate magna cum laude and head to law school. And from there, he had boldly declared, he planned to become the first black man to reside at 1600 Pennsylvania Avenue. Ronny had been an intellectual thinker in the mold of a young Cornel West, which was remarkable considering his impoverished background and humble upbringing. He had majored in philosophy with dreams of radically shifting those paradigms and ideologies that, in his mind, kept the majority of black America still enslaved in a poverty mentality.

And Jermaine . . . well, he was the communications major destined to be a media star, what with a voice that rivaled the bass tones of Barry White, the smoothness of Billy Dee Williams, and the pronunciation and diction of Bryant Gumbel. "Golden" was what his voice had been nicknamed and aptly labeled by a reporter with the *Washington Post* who had heard Jermaine emcee a student NAACP fund-raiser during his senior year at Howard. The moniker had stuck.

"Here I am, the man with the golden voice guaranteed to get you excited and inspired about life," he stated aloud, laughing in derision as he mocked his own announcer. Truthfully, it would have been more realistic for him to think of Eric as still being alive and being elected president of the United States than to think he could provide inspiration for his own life just then.

Tears rolled down his cheeks as he watched the stars twinkle and dance with each other in the moonlit sky above the city of angels. He was already feeling the numbing sensations of a hangover pushing its way into his brain even though it wasn't even two o'clock in the morning. And he hadn't drunk heavily in years; the last time he even recalled having a hangover was at a college party when it was still fashionable for brothers to sport flat-top haircuts.

Shoulda been me and not you, Eric. That nostalgic thought was true about so many things. *Shoulda been me in that car and not you. You would've had my vote to be president . . .*

chapter three

"OKAY, XAVIER, I'M on my way. They held me up with the rental car but everything's fine now," Myra shouted into her cell phone as she passed underneath an airport tunnel. The grating combination of the static and the phone's poor reception was getting on her nerves, so she decided to put a quick end to this conversation. Besides, talking while driving was a habit she was striving to correct.

"Remind me to talk to Cindy, though, about making sure the company credit card is current, okay? Peace and blessings." She clicked off her cell as she headed west along the beltway, heading for Interstate 45. The first time Myra had visited the city of Houston, it had been on a business trip while she was still working for corporate America. Though that had been years ago, she had still remembered the city's near-stifling summer humidity that had caused her to sweat in places she hadn't thought possible. That unpleasant memory was blazingly brought back to life once she had stepped off the plane a few hours ago and felt a blast of furnace-like air that seemed to take away even the moisture in her mouth. Though she was Georgia born and raised and therefore accustomed to occasional high temperatures, she had a hard time believing that over two and a half million people would live in *this* kind of heat.

"Maybe they know something I don't," she thought.

An hour and a half later, she finally pulled up in the driveway of the plush two-story home in the southwest suburb of Sugarland. She had noticed that most of the homes' yards were not that large in square footage, like she was accustomed to seeing back in Atlanta. The majority of the lots here seemed to be situated almost on top of one another, although that was not the case with the mansion sprawling before her. The white and beige brick house sat back a good ways from the street in the center of a large cul-de-sac, seeming to tower over the rest of the neighborhood's homes in a stately fashion. Small azaleas, red tulips, and purple chrysanthemums lined the walkway and circled around the three large trees in a well-tended path to the front doors. The lush green grass was professionally trimmed and edged around the same path, reminding Myra of the landscaping normally reserved for golf courses at posh country clubs.

You've done good for yourself, girl . . .

She rang the doorbell twice, hearing the reverberating chime faintly echo throughout the house. The door opened not long afterward, revealing a slender, petite young woman wearing a light blue knit polo and khaki capri pants. Myra immediately recognized the writer from the photo inserts she had on file.

"Hello, Miss Clark. I'm Myra Washington, editor-in-chief of *Song of Solomon* magazine." After noting the somewhat blank expression being given off by Candace, Myra promptly continued. "Um, I arranged an interview through your publicist, Carl Daniels, but I—"

"Oh, yes!" Recognition now came to the writer's face. "Yes, I remember now. Carl sent me the e-mail on that but I didn't get confirmation on the time."

"Oh, I see." Myra fidgeted with the strap on her bag. She suddenly felt awkward, like a door-to-door peddler with out-of-date goods nobody wants. She cleared her throat and willed herself to remain confident. "Well . . . if this is a bad time, I completely understand."

"No, no. Of course not," Candace answered, seemingly sensing Myra's discomfort. With an inviting smile, she opened the door farther and beckoned for Myra to come inside. "The least I can do is get you in from that heat. It's not even summer yet and already it's humid enough to dry out a weave."

Myra self-consciously smoothed down her hair. "Girl, I know that's the truth."

Candace led Myra through the foyer, past the den, and into the airy sunroom. "Please, have a seat on the couch. I'll be ready in a sec—let me just run and forward my calls to voice mail."

"Oh, go right ahead." Myra took advantage of the time to allow herself a long look around the sunroom's decor and furnishings, especially appreciating the colorful painting of the woman with the Bible, gazing toward Heaven. The old woman sort of reminded her of her own grandmother, who had been a mighty woman of God in her own right. She smiled to herself as she thought, *"Strong spiritual heritage runs in the family. . . ."*

She guessed correctly that the white leather couch would be luxurious to sit on, and while making herself comfortable, she refreshingly took in the aromatics of the room. The blend of French vanilla candles and assorted potpourri was pleasantly enlivening to her senses after braving all kinds of toxic smells at the airport. She opened her notebook portfolio, full of all the information Xavier had felt she needed to make her pitch to land a writer of Candace Clark's talent.

Okay, God, You've let me come this far. This is such an awesome opportunity . . . I'm just going to trust You now . . .

Candace walked back in the room a few minutes later. "Myra, I'm so sorry—I just don't know where my manners are right now. My mother taught me better than that, I can promise you. Can I offer you something to drink? Coffee? Tea?"

"Oh no, thank you," Myra answered. "I imagine our roles are kind of reversed right now. I mean, I'm sure that you've orchestrated a lot of interviews before. And it's been a long time since I've done one; I usually just oversee the operations and production of the magazine."

"I admire and applaud you for that, you know," Candace commented as she settled down in the large easy chair across from Myra. "Because we need some more women—black women at that—in management positions in journalism. And in media across the board, for that matter. Sure, all the large studios can hire pretty talking heads and fill their quotas all they want, but the job that you're doing is where the real power lies—ownership."

Amen to that . . . Myra smiled graciously and twirled her Mont Blanc fountain pen around on her fingers, unsure of how to begin. She had never before considered herself to be an excellent seller of anything, but that was precisely what she was here to do.

"Candace, this isn't . . . oh, how can I say it? This probably isn't going to be a typical interview."

Again, Candace offered an understanding smile. "I sort of realized that."

"You did?"

She nodded, still smiling. "Well, you were right when you said that I've orchestrated a lot of interviews. Goodness, I've probably spent the better part of the last three years running around getting quotes from people. Girl, I could tell you some stories!" Her smile quickly turned into unabashed laughter. "Anyway, I guess I've done enough interviewing to know that nice fountain pen you're twirling around may look wonderful, but a Mont Blanc is normally not the pen of choice for writing shorthand and taking notes. If you were also tape-recording, then using a pen like that might be alright, though I still wouldn't advise it."

Myra placed her pen on the table in front of her and folded her hands in her lap. Now wasn't that something, she thought to herself—being accurately and openly read like a newspaper headline by a woman half her age.

"Well, just call me an amateur, then; I haven't interviewed in years! You're right, Candace—I didn't exactly come to get quotes from you or take a lot of notes. The truth of the matter is that I came to make a . . . a pitch. I'm sure you know that Mario Jordan wants only you to do the upcoming feature on Jermaine Hill."

At that statement, Candace wearily shook her head like a girl who's received one too many flowers from a boy she doesn't like. "Yes, I've gotten more than my share of messages from Super Mario in the past week, so I guess I'm going to be the one to do this. But let me tell you, I'm not exactly falling over myself to write this piece."

"Really? Well, that's news to me. Jermaine Hill is one of the hottest celebrities in the nation right now."

"Yeah, that's what everyone says."

"But not you?"

Candace shrugged and showed indifference. "I'm not saying that. I just don't exactly see what makes him so hot."

"Candace, you do have to admit he does look . . . what's the word nowadays? I know people don't say *handsome* anymore."

Candace laughed. "Watch out now, Myra—you're telling your age! Yes, he is *fine*, as they say. But looks aren't everything. And to me, the whole thing just happened overnight, it seems. Who even knew about him two years ago? Which goes to show that fame has a lot to do with opportunity and . . . well . . . a little bit of . . ."

"A little bit of luck," Myra finished. "Not that I put any stock in luck myself, just for the record. But I do believe in opportunity. That's why I'm here, to tell you the truth. I'm here because of an opportunity. Candace, you've established yourself as a first-rate columnist, meaning you can write for any publication you choose. And like I said earlier, I'm here to make a pitch."

Candace raised her eyebrows a little and leaned back in her chair.

"I'm not sure that you know a whole lot about the vision we have or that you even read our magazine, to be honest. This is just a little background info, all of which is in a portfolio I have for you, but in the past year we gained fifteen percent of the market share for our demographic. We're also showing that we have a broader appeal to the readers of not only urban magazines, but also of mainstream publications that are not particularly African-American. In Atlanta, we—"

She abruptly stopped, suddenly realizing that all she was doing was reciting and spouting out the facts and specs Xavier had provided for her. If this was the best she was going to do, she might as well just have faxed the data sheet and saved a long, hot, humid trip.

Oh no, I'm not. I didn't get my hair messed up in this humidity after driving almost two hours to not go all out for this chance . . . God, help me here . . . "Candace, I . . . I could give you all the facts, surveys, and studies showing that all we're really lacking is the exclusive rights to one major national story that would take us to the front of the urban market share. That's what I believe, at any rate. Because when it's all said and done, it's all about the readers."

"Absolutely. I can definitely agree with that."

"We're relatively new—*Song of Solomon* is just three years old—so we don't yet have the established readers like magazines that have been around for much longer do, and I understand that. But don't think that I'm not jumping at every chance I see to put our name out there where a larger number of people can see it. I guess it's kind of like my granny used to tell me when I was a little gal growing up in Macon—you ain't no better than nobody else, but ain't nobody else better than you."

Candace smiled. "That's funny. I had an aunt that used to tell me the very same thing."

Leaning forward a little on the couch, Myra continued, "You know, when I started this magazine, I didn't have a whole lot of formal training. There was no one to show me what to do or what not to do. All I was holding on to was the dream I first had at Spelman to someday run a magazine that focused on the issues of our people, and do so with moral integrity and a spirit of excellence. And that dream was toughened over twenty years working in corporate America and raising a son by myself, let me tell you. Since starting *Song of Solomon,* I've been waiting for an opportunity just like this to come my way, so when it did, I couldn't get down here fast enough to talk to you. Mario Jordan has stated that he wants you to be the one to interview Jermaine Hill. But neither he nor you has indicated *which* magazine will be publishing the interview. So I came down here because . . . well, because I would very much like you to write the feature with us, with *Song of Solomon.*"

Candace nodded her head slowly like she had foreknown what was going to be said. "As you know, Myra, I am a freelancer, so it's not my nature to sign a contract with any one magazine."

"Yes, I am aware of that. We wouldn't ask you to

sign a contract or have any obligations other than for this feature."

Candace nodded again. For a moment she was silent, seemingly lost in thought as she absently rubbed the face on her watch. "Myra, I'm afraid all I'm able to tell you right now is that I will have to get back to you with my response." She held up her hands in a show of mock defense. "I know, I know, that sounds like the usual run-around answer, but I will definitely be contacting you within the week on the decision. My publicist is working with Mario Jordan right now on an itinerary for Mr. Hill and as soon as they have the dates, a magazine will be announced."

"I see. Well, can you at least tell me what will be factored into the decision?" Myra wasn't grasping for straws just yet but she hadn't come all the way to Houston to not dig up as much information as she possibly could.

"Yes. Of course we'll be looking at the overall distribution numbers and the target demographics. And there will be other criteria that . . . how can I say it? That . . . aren't as easily quantified." She looked directly at Myra.

Myra saw a slight, reassuring smile cross the young woman's face. Or maybe she was just imagining that she had seen one.

chapter four

THE TUNE THAT Bell was singing this morning was one of those old Negro spirituals that were somehow becoming easier and easier for the saints of God to forget. But not for her, even with her Alzheimer's disease. She probably stood no chance of ever forgetting because her great-granny, granny, and mother had all sung the same thing in her hearing for as long as she could remember. And though Bell used to loathe that somewhat depressing-sounding melody, wouldn't you know—she now found *herself* walking around telling Mary not to weep and Martha not to moan. Funny, that thing called life.

"Don't you be forgettin' God, Bell honey," her mother would tell her nearly every day as she hummed and sang in the tradition of their ancestors—no matter if she was braiding Bell's hair, washing the pots and pans, or steam-ironing those long, billowy dresses that Bell used to hate wearing. Bell knew better than to complain though—she learned quickly that any extra lip granted her a stinging slap across that same mouth.

"You sassin' me, missy?"

That's just how it had been in the Davis house—theirs was a sanctified family of holy rollers and tongue talkers who went to church just about every day of the week.

"Don't you be forgettin' God . . ." And she had not. Nor would she let Jermaine forget about Him, either.

"Saa-aavve my so-on, oh God . . ."

• • •

THE LIVELY RADIO ANNOUNCER began his much-hyped introduction of the Jermaine Hill show, ending with his typical directive for America's people to turn up their radios as loud as possible.

Candace balked at turning up the volume as loud as possible, but she did nudge the sound up a bit on her car's stereo as she waited for a notoriously long red light to turn green at an intersection in the Medical Center district. She had just picked up a suit from her tailor in the Village and was now on her way to Rice University to finish an article she was working on for the M. D. Anderson hospital system. Although she was a celebrated alum now, she still found writing in the university's library perfect for her, particularly when penning pieces for the medical field. She could picture the stately, ivy-covered buildings that were gloriously alive with academic brilliance and wisdom permeating their historic walls.

She had been drawn to Rice eight years earlier during her initial visit. Rice had been the first school to offer her a full scholarship—she had gone to the open house only because it had given her a wonderful excuse to leave home for a weekend. It was a mere four-hour drive from Highland Park, the upscale Dallas suburb where she had been raised, to Houston.

So it had come as a huge surprise when she had immediately taken to the school's quaint atmosphere and student life. And although Rice was generally not known for a strong journalism program, one of its professors, Dr. West, had immediately offered to mentor Candace after reading one of her features written while she was still in high school. Dr. West, in a twist of incredible fortune for Candace, just happened to be a Sunday features editor with the *Houston Chronicle*. Consequently, much of Candace's vital hands-on training during her tenure at Rice had come from working with the veteran editor at the *Chronicle*, and she was grateful and indebted to Dr. West for all her successes.

"This is Jermaine Hill once again coming to you live with an OD of inspiration for your soul. How's everybody doing out there?"

"Just fine, Mr. Hill, just fine . . ." Candace responded aloud to herself. Already, she had begun a preliminary outline of some questions she had in mind to ask Jermaine, thanks in large part to always listening to Tasha's ravings. Tasha had now taken to outlandishly proclaiming herself president of the Jermaine Hill Fan Club.

Tasha, you need help, sistah girl. Professional help, preferably.

Most of her questions so far were open-ended, as she imagined she would just give the man plenty of room and freedom to talk and see what happened.

Seemed that's what he did best, anyway. She was scheduled to fly out to L.A. for the interview in a few days, and although she was flattered that Mario Jordan had stated that he would work only with her, in a way she was still a bit uninterested in the whole affair. Celebrity scoops and tabloid journalism weren't exactly her thing. She had built her name and reputation thus far writing solid, informational, and morally conscious pieces that tended to linger in the minds of her readers long after the last words were read. Still, though, she took some solace in the fact that she, as always, would be professional and honest. She would strive to give an objective, untainted view of this man whom the whole nation was talking about. Her personal ideas and opinions wouldn't even come forth; she would simply be an observant, note-taking, celebrity-following shadow.

"Let's get today started off with talking about love," Jermaine continued on the radio. "Lovin' what you do and doin' what you love. Because isn't that what it's all about? A lot of people always complain about what they have to put up with on their nine to five. I have to ask these people, is it worth it to waste eight hours of your day at a place doing something or being around people who wear constantly on your nerves?"

Be realistic, Jermaine. Most people work their jobs simply because they have to. Have to eat, pay rent . . .

"And I know what you are saying to that—you're saying be realistic, Jermaine. You've got to work if you want to eat."

Candace raised an eyebrow and her mouth almost curved into a small smile. Almost.

"But is that what our life has come down to? Work,

sleep, eat. Work, sleep, eat. You get ahead on the right only to fall behind on your left. You get a raise, you buy a bigger car. You win some money in the stock market, you buy a bigger house. But then you have to keep working to pay for and keep all those bigger material possessions, and a lot of times you end up like a duck trying to swim."

A duck?

"You ever seen a duck swim? It's kind of like some of our lives. We're trying to look smooth and unruffled on the top, but we're furiously paddling those feet beneath the surface just to keep our heads above water. And in the end, we ask ourselves whether it was really worth all the trouble in the first place. But Jermaine is here to tell you that it can be worth it, if you do what you love and love what you do."

That's kind of a simple approach to take . . .

"I know, I know, it sounds simple."

This time, a rather convincing smile found its way to Candace's face.

"And the realists again are going to be calling in and writing to the show, telling me that it's easier said than done. But I also know that you only live this life once, and you have to live it with no regrets. You feel me? So let's talk about this some more. And let Jermaine give you some simple suggestions . . ."

He continued speaking, but Candace switched off the radio as she turned from Greenbriar onto the large parking lot behind Rice Stadium. Much of what the man was saying surprisingly made sense to her, causing her to briefly wonder why she hadn't listened to the show before. Probably because she, jokingly, had teased Tasha so much about swooning over celebrities that she involuntarily had made up her mind not to even listen to Jermaine Hill. To her, he was just another one of Tasha's boys, sadly meaning that he was doomed to be featured on one of *Entertainment Tonight*'s "Whatever Happened to . . ." segments. Of course, that was before she had been literally hand-picked to do this interview last week. That small fact had changed everything. Now, she was not only going to have to listen to his shows, but she would also have to do some more research about him to give her interview credibility.

Turning off the ignition, she pulled out her cell phone from her bag. Since meeting with the editor of *Song of Solomon* yesterday afternoon, she had been mulling over an idea that had originated in her head and was now curiously making its way into her heart.

You know you should do this . . . when was the last time you talked to Daddy, anyway?

Since her mother's death six years ago, Candace and her father had grown a little distant. Harold Clark had relocated to his hometown of Longview, Texas, after Analee had passed, and Candace now saw him only during the holidays. If then, even. When she was growing up, her father had been the breadwinner of the family. And he did so while personifying the strong, silent type—he was never one to openly express his feelings with his wife and daughter. But not once could Analee or Candace ever question if his priorities were in the right place. His love for them had been shown by the fact that he had come home every night from his lucrative engineering job. Papa was no rolling stone.

And in the later stages of Analee's battle with cancer, he had spent every minute that he possibly could at his wife's bedside.

Last Thanksgiving, when Candace had gone to visit him, she had taken note of several *Song of Solomon* magazines on the coffee table.

"I didn't know you subscribed to this," she had commented.

"Oh, I guess I'm just trying to get back in touch with my roots, Candi," he had replied. "When you get a little older and things begin to happen to you in a way you never thought, well you just never thought could, you start to reevaluate what's important."

Harold's father had been a Baptist preacher from the South, the son of two generations of Baptist preachers before him. Candace always had supposed the pressure of becoming a man of the cloth like his forefathers had not sat well with her father, whereas the academic pressures he had experienced while pursuing his engineering degree had sat extremely well with him. All those hypotheses, theories, and scientific evidence had caused him to question the authenticity and meaning of Christianity in his life, and the results had not been pretty. He had walked out of his father's church one Sunday in 1952 and had not looked back.

Remembering what her father had said about getting in touch with his roots, she now dialed her father's number.

"Daddy? Hey, it's Candi."

"Candi?" Her father's surprise was genuine, she knew. It was not her normal routine to call him during the day just to keep in touch and let him know how she was doing. Like a typical writer, she preferred sending letters.

"It's good to hear your voice, sweetheart. Is everything alright?"

"Yes, yes, everything's fine."

"Well, I just asked because you usually don't call . . ."

Candace laughed. "I know, Daddy. But you never know, I may call more often if they keep raising the price of stamps." She laughed again. "Listen, I have a quick question for you. Do you still subscribe to *Song of Solomon*? You know, the whole getting back in touch with your roots thing?"

"My roots, hmm?" He was silent for a moment. "Yes, I still subscribe. The articles are really something else, you know? It's . . . they . . . they've been helping me."

"Good. I'm . . . well, I'm glad to hear that." Talking about faith and spiritual issues was still difficult for them, she could see. So perhaps she could do something about this difficulty, something that might be the first step along the path to change.

"Well, Daddy, make sure you check out next month's issue real closely, okay? There might be something in there that . . . that . . ." she was unsure of how to finish what she wanted to say. She was much better at expressing herself in writing.

"I'll be sure to check it out, sweetheart," he cut in, to Candace's relief.

• • •

AMBROSE RIVERS WAS A complicated, oft-misunderstood man. Truth be told, most people thought he was plain crazy. But in his mind, he knew that he was not a mental case. The California Department of Corrections, however, had ruled otherwise and instructed him to be placed in Atascadero State Hospital eight months ago. Needless to say, it had been the worst eight months of his fifty-six years.

Prior to all this coming about, he had dutifully and tirelessly traveled the country as an itinerant evangelist, speaking charismatically at small churches, open-air tent crusades, and generally anywhere he was able to procure a crowd. The term *crowd* being relative, of course, because to him just two people would rightly define an audience to his liking. With a boldness and fire that invoked a measure of either fear or horror in the hearts of the people he preached to, he unashamedly called for repentance in a modern-day society where sin was rampant. Because of this unpopular message, his words were generally met with disdain and the unsympathetic raising of eyebrows, even among people who called themselves "Christians." Not that he particularly cared, though. He thought of himself as a modern-day John the Baptist.

And the forerunner of Jesus Christ had his own share of haters, too . . .

With no family to speak of after being raised as a ward of the state, he had drifted through the California public school system without ever receiving a diploma. Again, not that he cared. By reading more books and literature than most college-educated businesspeople, he possessed a high level of enlightenment, along with a burning passion for calling God's children back to the Father's love—all in all, a dangerous combination.

The LAPD, however, had believed Ambrose to be a danger to society in other ways, finally arresting him on a disturbance of the peace charge after one of his typical "sermons" outside a Hollywood television studio. The misdemeanor would have been dismissed by the studio's executive if he had agreed never to set foot within five hundred feet of the property, but Ambrose wasn't giving up any ground.

"Everywhere the soles of my feet tread, the land is mine," he had emphatically argued in court. "And I refuse to be told where I may or may not step!"

The State of California thought otherwise. After various members of both the religious and psychiatric communities had performed tests on Ambrose, he had been ordered to undergo treatment at Atascadero.

Now, Ambrose paced firmly back and forth in his enclosed room, beads of sweat popping out on his forehead as he preached to no one in particular.

"And I will rain upon him, and upon his hands, and upon the many people that are with him, an overflowing rain, and great hailstones, fire and brimstone!" Ambrose now emphatically declared, his voice echoing loudly throughout the empty room. The inflection of his voice, as it rose and fell upon the thrust of every other word, eerily mimicked the preaching style of the late Martin Luther King Jr.

"Thus I will magnify myself, and sanctify myself and I will be known in the eyes of many nations, and they shall know that I am the Lord!"

"Shut up, crazy prophet wannabe!" came a voice from just outside the closed door. "Preach with your mouth closed! Mouth closed . . . mouth closed . . .

mouth closed . . ." The phrase-repetition gave away the identity of the annoying voice. Ambrose knew his name to be Johnny Lee, and during the past months it had become his personal mission to open Johnny's spiritually blinded eyes.

"The kingdom of Heaven suffereth violence, and the vio-o-lent take it by force!" Ambrose responded. "I claim your soul in the name of the Father, the Son, and—"

"Preach with your mouth closed! I don't wanna hear you . . . can't hear you . . . don't wanna hear you! Mouth closed, mouth closed . . ." Johnny Lee was wailing now in a childlike sing-song voice that Ambrose would have thought funny if the poor fool's soul hadn't been at stake.

As the two men's voices became louder, each one refusing to give the other the last word, the sound of rubber-soled shoes padding along linoleum tiles was soon heard. The security personnel were coming to restore order to this wing—it would not do to have the entire floor riled up in a debate over the coming of the kingdom of Heaven. Again.

• • •

LATER THAT EVENING, Candace finally made the call to her publicist after giving her burgeoning idea some further thought. Because after all, what difference did it make which magazine carried the story? And so what if *Song of Solomon* was a Christian-based publication? What was the problem with that? Who would know of her personal reasons to write for them besides her and her father?

This is what happens after you've paid your dues . . . freedom is a wonderful thing . . .

"Candi, am I hearing you right?" Apparently, though, Carl wasn't in much agreement with her strange idea of *freedom.* "Are you telling me that you want to write this story, which I might remind you is bigger than Oprah interviewing Michael Jackson, bigger than Halle and Denzel winning Oscars on the same night, bigger than—"

"The point has been made already," she interrupted with a hint of irritation. Carl was an excellent publicist, but he could be a drama king sometimes, prone to making a huge show out of just about anything. All things considered, however, she supposed that was an acceptable bad habit for a PR man to have.

"But this story is that big, that groundbreaking, and you want to write it for . . . for . . . what was the name again?"

"*Song of Solomon.*"

"Song of . . . hold on, isn't that the name of a Toni Morrison novel?" With a bit of sarcasm, he began chuckling.

Candace shook her head and tightly clenched the phone in her hand, wishing Carl was in front of her so she could give his shoulders and neck a good shaking. She never ceased to find it amusing that she, at a shade over five feet six, was a good three inches taller than him.

"It's also the name of a book in the Bible. And it's the name of that new urban magazine based out of

Atlanta. You should know who they are quite well, Carl. You just arranged an interview with their editor and me."

"Yeah, well maybe I shouldn't have," he muttered in response. "And I wouldn't have, if I knew that woman was going to influence you to make a decision like this. Candace, I know you're not the biggest fan of Jermaine Hill, okay? I know that. But this is the biggest celebrity story so far of the twenty-first century! You don't want to blow it on an unknown."

"Carl, this is *not* the biggest story."

"It is!"

"Even if it is," she continued, wishing she could now throw something at him in addition to shaking his neck, "I don't see why this is such a problem. If I remember correctly from our last meeting, Mario Jordan said all he was concerned about was that I do the feature. There wasn't a stipulation on which magazine. You said yourself that was something that could be decided by me."

"Yes, but Candi, a story as big as this needs the kind of advertising and distribution to put it in every major bookstore, grocery checkout aisle, Mom-and-Pop convenience store, and newsstand in the country."

"*Song of Solomon*'s distribution and printing numbers are comparable with other magazines in our target demographic," she countered. "I can fax you their asset sheet if you want to take a look at it. I have, and can tell you that I'm very impressed with their figures. Besides, I've got a good feeling about their editor and their overall vision."

"A good feeling?" Carl sounded incredulous.

"Don't knock feelings, honey. Or a writer's gut instinct, for that matter. And as far as advertising is concerned, it shouldn't be a big problem if this Jermaine Hill is as big as you're making him out to be."

Candace heard Carl sigh in exasperation. "Candi, I don't understand. I don't get it. Why *Song of Solomon*? You've never written for them before. You've got great contacts and established readers with four leading magazines. But you want to write the biggest celebrity story in recent history for an unknown magazine? In my opinion, that doesn't make sense at all. And that is what you pay me for, right? My professional opinion."

"I pay you to publicize the stories and books that I write. And I do appreciate your professional opinion, Carl. But in this case, it doesn't matter which magazine gets the story. The guy's name alone is going to create a firestorm of publicity." She paused a moment, silently relishing her momentum, before adding, "and remember my instincts about this."

Her publicist sighed again in what Candace took to be the first sign of defeat. She had known he would soon give in. What choice did he have? For all the wonderful things he could do, the pecking order still showed her to be on top.

The pen is still mightier than the sword . . . "So, you're going to get the necessary papers over to Myra Washington and set everything up?"

"You're killing me, Candi," he groaned. "You know that? Just stick a fork in me, 'cause I'm done already."

"Oh, Carl," she replied, laughing. "No more drama for tonight, alright? This story's going to work no matter who prints it and you know it. Now if you and

Mario Jordan want to keep your star writer happy, then you'll indulge me and go along with this simple request."

"Stick a fork in me, Candi . . ."

"I know, I know, because you're done," she finished. "Carl, I don't know why you're so down about this. Think Halle and Denzel, okay?" She couldn't help the insinuating snicker that escaped her lips.

"Oh, you're a comedienne now? Keep your day job, Miss Thing. But since you brought those stars up, I haven't seen any of them do anything for *Song of Solomon*."

"Actually, *you* brought them up, drama king. And you're thinking too small with them, anyway." Her laughter was beyond constraint now. "Think Candace Clark!" She hung up the phone then, wondering when she last had laughed so hard. Poor Carl. She'd have to remember to send him a Hallmark card. Preferably a small, short one.

chapter five

THE EVENING SUN SETTING just over the crest of the Santa Monica mountains cast subtle reddish-orange and faded yellow hues along the sprawling horizon of Los Angeles, signaling the coming end to another day. The windowpane Jermaine was blankly staring through was a brilliant kaleidoscope of colors as it reflected nature's glory, but he was blind to the beauty and splendor of it all. He was blind to a lot of things at the moment. Yesterday, after taping the radio show, he had been out at a mansion in Malibu all night, partying with people he neither knew, nor really cared to know. But it had beat the miserable alternative—staying home and conjuring up new methods for ending his life.

"Alright, J, listen up," Mario Jordan continued, now pacing back and forth along the wine-and-rose-colored Axminster carpet in the building's executive conference room. He had taken off his wingtips an hour ago in an effort to save the designer carpet from extra wear and tear. "We're down to the last two items on the agenda."

His agent had just gone through five previous items on the current week's agenda, but the information had run through Jermaine's head like water off a duck's back. Mario had discussed the new proposals from media outlets rivaling KKTL's offer, then had talked about Jermaine's scheduled weekend appearances at Magic Johnson's golf tournament raising money for AIDS research and at the red-carpet premiere of the new Steven Spielberg film at Mann's Chinese Theatre. It wasn't that long ago that Jermaine had been thrilled to meet the stars he had grown up admiring and idolizing. But he had soon found out that people were all the same, no matter who they were. It was like his Aunt Bell used to tell him, "ev'rybody got to put they's pants on one leg at a time."

"J, how can I say this?" Mario glanced up at the ceiling, his forehead now creased with several worry lines. His gaze when he looked back at Jermaine a few seconds later was direct and sure. "You've got to stop picking up these women at these parties, bottom line. You're not an up-and-coming star anymore who can go around sleeping with every fine thing in a skirt. You're definitely on the A-list now and that means you've got a big target on your back. Don't think for a minute that these women don't see it. You hearing me, J?"

Jermaine had become a master at tuning out people and conversations that he wasn't particularly interested in. He now blinked his eyes twice, slowly realizing his agent was looking squarely at him and expecting an answer.

"Yeah, Mario, yeah. Whatever."

"Well, you'd better be because the last thing we

need is for some gold digger to claim you're her baby's daddy," Mario continued. He cleared his throat then, looking away for a moment. "I shouldn't have to even ask this . . . but, uh, you are using protection, right?"

Jermaine immediately stopped tuning the conversation out, very much awake now. His nonchalance quickly turned into a simmering anger.

"What the—! What kind of question is that, am I using protection? I'm not paying you to be my father!"

"J, I'm just looking out for your best interests. And the last time I checked, you *are* paying me to do *that.*" Mario took a seat in his chair. His hands, smooth and finely manicured, now ran back and forth over his sleek, bald head. "Listen, are you okay? I mean, is everything alright with you?"

"Whaddya mean, is everything alright? You schedule my interviews, negotiate my contracts, handle my business. You should know if everything's alright."

"I'm not talking about business now."

"What else would you be talking about?"

Mario pointed his finger at Jermaine. "You."

"Tell me something I don't know, Sherlock." His anger was boiling now—it was the constant meetings, the contracts, the autograph sessions, the paparazzi following him around—it was all reaching the breaking point. "That's what this meeting is about, just like every meeting we have. It's about me, Mario. Me. The new cable show, the contracts, who I'm dating, who I need to be dating. I'm living in a fishbowl, Mario. Don't you get it? Feed me once a day, listen to my golden voice, and tap the bowl twice if you feel so inclined."

Mario sighed. "See, that's exactly what I'm talking about, J. You're not yourself. And you haven't been for the last month or so."

"I'm not myself? I'm not myself!" His voice grew louder with every breath. "How would you know if I was or wasn't myself?" He cursed loudly. "You've been my agent for what, like nine months, and you're telling me you already know everything there is to know about me!"

"Listen, *you* were the one who came to me nine months ago to represent you, remember? *You* were the one who told me about your dreams and goals, how you wanted to be the most famous, most-listened-to motivational speaker in America. And look at what we've been able to do together! You've got major corporations scheduling their lunch break around your radio program. You've got the best crossover marketing appeal to all races and social classes in this nation since Air Jordan in his prime. You're a hero to inner-city, single-parent homes. You're—"

"Spare me the bugle-and-drum routine, Mario. I know what we've accomplished."

"And we can do so much more, J. But you're not a machine. You're a human being like everyone else. So you can try to hide whatever's going on with you from everybody else, but you're not fooling me. I can tell something's not right." He rubbed his hands together. "And whatever's not right, we need to get it right before your interview."

Back to business so quickly, is that it? Back to Jermaine in the fishbowl . . .

"We need to get it right," Mario persisted. "Because

I really do care about what's going on with you. Behind the scenes, I mean."

Then, as quickly as the fury had risen up within Jermaine, inexplicably it now dissipated back into a state of hopeless indifference. Or indifferent hopelessness, perhaps. It wasn't that he didn't have the fortitude to stay angry, it was just that he really didn't care anymore. In his thoughts, he was now somewhere back on the coastal highway overlooking the Pacific Ocean. And then he was driving off the cliff, down into the blue nothingness that awaited him. No longer was the fish in the fishbowl. The fish was now in the ocean, free to swim however he pleased . . .

"J, are you hearing me?"

"Yeah, Mario, yeah. Whatever."

Mario sighed yet again, then continued. "We lined up Candace Clark to write the feature. As you know, she's the best in the business."

Ah yes, the business . . .

"It's a funny thing, though. Her agent tells me Candace is adamant about that new magazine *Song of Solomon* publishing the interview. If I'm not mistaken, they're a Christian-based magazine. I know you touch on Judeo-Christian principles in your motivational talks, but you don't claim any specific religious background to your approach." He shifted himself in his chair. "Do you have any qualms about them printing this interview? Because if you do, we can go with someone else. However adamant she may be about using them, I'm sure we could persuade her to use another publication."

Like it matters, Sherlock . . . "They're fine. Whatever."

"Alright, I'll call her people and let them know." He slid his wingtips back on his feet and stood up. "That's all I have on the agenda, J. Take my advice—you go home and get some rest. That's probably all you need, anyway."

Jermaine nodded. "Yeah, you're probably right." *You've never been so wrong, Mario my man . . .*

"And J?"

"Hmm?"

"No more parties and no more strange girls. I mean that."

"Yeah, okay." *Whatever.*

chapter six

CHANTAL DIXON WAS ALWAYS the first one from her investigative team to arrive at StarWatch studios in the mornings. Phil, the security guard, nodded politely and laughed to himself as Chantal carefully passed him, using both hands to precariously balance her purse, cardkey, laptop case, and steaming cup of coffee. It was an act worthy of Ringling Bros., Phil was fond of saying. She made it safely to her desk and set the foam cup down gingerly on a multitude of scattered papers strewn atop her desk. She paid no mind to her purse and computer case as they dropped to the floor, for her attention was solely fixed on her monitor. Silently, she cursed at how long it actually took to start the thing. Slow technology and slow people had no place in the life of someone forever teetering on the slope between impatience and intolerance.

Chantal had started her investigative career ten years ago in the same manner as had everyone else in the field—as a gopher. It was an unenviable job, but all positions in the media industry went the way of the tenured totem pole. Dues simply had to be paid.

Chantal had put in her time at Fox Sports in Houston, working the graveyard shift as a master control operator. That had been two years of absolute boredom, but the people she met and experiences she dealt with had proven to be invaluable. She learned the insider knowledge one simply didn't pick up by merely taking college communication courses. It was on to the Dallas CBS affiliate after that, where she honed her investigative skills and developed the relationships she would soon be using on a larger platform.

Not long afterward, her big break had come while on a business trip to California. Like most people, she was drawn to celebrity sightings so she had taken a short detour in her business itinerary to take in the 74th annual Academy Awards ceremony. She managed to gain entrance to the press area from an industry contact she had kept in good relations with from her days at Fox. Operating as a freelancer and having the time of her life, she was able to get exclusive soundbites and quotes from key black entertainers discussing the historical significance of Halle Berry and Denzel Washington receiving Oscars on the same night. *StarWatch News* had been quick to hire her before E! or *Entertainment Tonight* could make an offer, and the proactive move had paid off handsomely for StarWatch. Since then, Chantal Dixon had firmly established her name and reputation as a reporter who delivered more dirt on the stars than anyone else in the business.

Her computer up and running now, she quickly accessed the e-mail she had been waiting for. The announcement of all the details for the Jermaine Hill interview was due to come out tomorrow, but she always got her information early.

"That doesn't make any sense," she murmured as she scanned the particulars highlighted in the e-mail. "How did *Song of Solomon* pull off something like that?"

Not that she needed any more kindling to stoke her already-flaming, red-hot fire of curiosity concerning all things pertaining to the guy with the golden voice. Jermaine Hill was the one star she had been unable to schedule an interview with since coming to StarWatch, in large part because Super Mario was still furious over a story she once wrote about the star speaker's alleged nightly trysts. Her information wasn't especially shocking since rumors of the man's playboy activities traveled all over Hollywood. Still, she had not been able to produce a confirmed source for that particular piece, a minor journalistic detail that Mario had not forgotten.

But this present e-mail, indicating Mario's incredible stipulation that Candace Clark would be the only one granted access to his star client, had further incensed Chantal. Candace Clark didn't even *write* celebrity stories, for crying out loud!

But if that was the way Super Mario wanted to play the game, so be it. Chantal was no lightweight, and she wasn't a novice either. In fact, in her opinion there was only one thing better than a story written about a well-liked celebrity. It was a *scandalous* story written about a well-liked celebrity. And if there was so much as a speck of dirt to be found, she was going to be the one to uncover it. And this time, she would have her confirmed source.

• • •

CANDACE KNEW WHAT unpleasantries awaited her as she opened her front door, so she was at least able to brace herself for the expected onslaught. Tasha had called earlier, saying she was coming over and Candace had better be there. As it happened, earlier in the day, Tasha had taken a message from Carl Daniels on Candace's cell phone. The only reason Tasha even had Candace's cell phone was because the battery in her own wireless had gone dead, and she had asked to borrow her friend's. No problem there, Candace had thought. What were friends for?

But the message Candace's publicist had for her was to confirm the airline and hotel for the trip to Los Angeles. Carl had no way of knowing Tasha was not to be in the loop on this—she was supposed to be the last one to know about the interview. The reason that Candace had been holding off telling her was, of course, because she knew, she just *knew*, that Tasha would be—

"Going off, Candi! I'm going off on you—how could you *not* tell me that you were the one to do this interview? I'm your best friend!" With a glare, she forcefully pushed her way past Candace and stormed toward the sunroom. "Or maybe you're one of those so-called friends who enjoys keeping secrets from the people who care about you the most."

"Tasha . . ." Candace rolled her eyes as she closed the door, knowing that uncontrollable emotional outbursts like this were exactly why she had planned to wait until the last minute to tell Tasha. Following her friend into the sunroom, she found Tasha seated at the bar, uncorking a bottle of sparkling cider.

"Tasha, you know I love you and everything, but I'm just going to be honest. I can't deal with how you carry on whenever the subject is Jermaine Hill."

"So you weren't going to tell me that you were the one conducting the interview? For weeks I get excited about this interview, and *my very own best friend* is the one who gets chosen to do it? And she doesn't think enough of me to even tell me?" Her eyes began bulging and Candace could make out that telltale vein popping out just below her jaw. She couldn't remember the last time she had seen Tasha so angry.

Candace fidgeted a little with her earring. "I was going to tell you . . ."

"When? When the story came out in print?"

"Well, probably a little bit just before that," she hesitantly began, "but that was my plan, yes."

"Why, Candi? I'm the president of his fan club!"

Oh Tasha, grow up . . . "The *unofficial* president of an *unofficial* fan club. And this is why I was going to wait to tell you, girlfriend. Because I knew you would give me no rest."

"You got that right I'd give you no rest! Candi, you know I'd give anything to be with that man! Jermaine Hill is like the . . . like the finest, most eligible bachelor around. He could be the one for me. Sometimes I don't understand you, you know? I mean, that you would keep something like this from me . . ." Her now-trembling voice trailed off, and Candace knew it was a matter of seconds before her friend would burst out with the tears.

Candace took the bottle from Tasha and filled a tumbler for herself. "Trust me, Tasha—I was just looking out for your own good. A guy like that is not the one for you."

Tasha's mouth dropped open. "How can you say something like that?"

Candace immediately regretted how she had phrased her last words. "Tasha, I . . . I didn't mean it like that. I just meant . . . well, I was just saying—"

"I know what you were saying. You don't think I could get a man like Jermaine. I'm not good enough, is that it?" The tears now began rolling down Tasha's cheeks.

"No, that's *not* what I meant. Tasha, you're my girl—you know that. I just don't want to see you hurt again." Keeping up with Tasha's constant man problems was like running a never-ending marathon in the heat of an African desert without drinking water. "It's not a good idea to start a relationship with a guy you practically keep on a pedestal. I mean, you worship the man like he's a god or something. So when Prince Charming turns out to be less than perfect, you're staring at a serious wake-up call."

"Is that so? Well, I guess *you* would know about wake-up calls where Prince Charming is concerned, now wouldn't you?"

Candace set her tumbler down firmly on the bar's countertop. "Let's not go there," she whispered.

An awkward silence ensued. Candace rubbed the end of her fingernail around the rim of the glass, wondering yet again why Tasha had to compartmentalize everything on either one end of the emotional extreme or the other. It had always been like that. From the first time they met while taking English Lit. at Rice ten years ago until now, Candace could have penned hundreds of soap opera pilots starring Tasha Briggs as the female lead.

Tasha dabbed at her wet, tear-streaked cheeks. “I’m sorry, Candi. I didn’t mean to bring up Ton—”

“I know,” she bluntly cut in, not wanting to even hear the name of that creep who had hurt her in what seemed like a lifetime ago. “No harm done.”

“It’s just that you’re going to be living with Jermaine Hill for two weeks!”

“I’m not going to be *living* with him, exactly,” she corrected. “Let’s keep the facts straight here.”

“You know what I mean. And you also know that I’d give anything to meet him. You could arrange for that to happen, right? Oh, c’mon, Caann-deee! If I were in your shoes I wouldn’t even have to think twice about it. Not for my best friend, I wouldn’t.”

If you were in my shoes, knowing you, you wouldn’t be thinking at all . . . “I’ll see what I can do, Tasha, but I’m not promising anything.”

The beaming smile on Tasha’s face, however, said otherwise.

“*Oh well . . . at least she’s not crying anymore . . .*” Candace thought. A major accomplishment in its own right.

• • •

“WE GOT THE STORY!” Myra jubilantly exclaimed, dancing a little jig in her kitchen as she celebrated with

Xavier over the phone. Her funky rendition of the *chicken* would have been hilarious to anyone watching her dance, but she was thankfully alone in her house.

"Didn't I tell you that Candace was known for accepting proposals from lesser-known magazines?"

Myra paused, trying to return her breathing and heart rate to normal. She couldn't remember the last time she had boogied with such fervor and meaning.

"Yes, but to sign with *us* for the biggest story of the year? Xavier, that's a miracle! It's nothing short of God answering our prayers. Oh, goodness," she added as her hand flew to her forehead. The full weight of what was now going to happen, business-wise, began to sink in. "We've got to dramatically increase our printing numbers. And our advertising rates have just skyrocketed, because I guarantee you we'll have no problem finding people who'll pay now. And we've got to double the distribution, and—"

"Whoa, Myra. You sound like my three-year-old daughter when you babble on like that," he said, chuckling. "Listen, this is not the time to get stressed out. If God dropped this in our lap then He'll grace us to handle the extra responsibilities."

"Yes. Yes, you're right." Myra started pacing her kitchen floor in circles. "But the demand for copies hot off the press is going to be like nothing we've seen, and there's no way we can let the early demand exceed our initial supply." *We've got to let people know that we're for real* . . . "I'm going to meet with our printer and core distributors this afternoon and then we'll have a conference call with the staff tonight. We've got to prep everyone on exactly what we're going to do."

"Myra?"

"Yes?"

"That brain of yours is shifting into editing overdrive, my friend. You know, it might be a good idea to have your pastor and prayer partners covering you even more in prayer. This is a huge, unprecedented venture we're undertaking, and we need to be sure that we're being led and guided in the right way."

Xavier, you're always pointing me back to prayer . . . "Thank you, Xavier. You're a spiritual beacon for this magazine. You always have been."

"I just do what I know how to do. And the rest I leave to God."

"Amen to that!" She thanked him once again and clicked off the phone. As she opened her laptop to begin penning the editor's note to the upcoming edition, she recalled her days at Spelman, when she had viewed the world through the eyes of hopeful idealism. She believed she was going to change the world. Most people at that impressionable, young period in life usually had such feelings, but she actually began to formulate a plan to do such an extraordinary thing.

That plan was going to be realized through the vehicle of mass media. For years, she strategized, brainstormed, plotted out proposals, and . . . *dreamed.* Oh, how she had dreamed. She envisioned a magazine that would not only inform her targeted audience about events and people in society, but would also cause the readers to reflect and ponder on the splendor and worth of a loving God. A modern day *Ebony* meets *Gospel Today* magazine.

Now, twenty years after the idea had been birthed in

her heart, she was discovering that dreams could indeed come true. The most anticipated celebrity interview in recent history had fallen to none other than *Song of Solomon*!

Myra's God was certainly an awesome God.

chapter seven

AS SHE SIPPED the cool and refreshing ginger ale, Candace tilted her head back against the comfortable leather headrest of the first-class seat and allowed herself a small smile. But this smile by no means adequately conveyed the silly, almost hysterical laughter bubbling inside her.

You've come a long way, sistah girl.

Hadn't she, though! She recalled how, as a child, she had been deathly afraid of airplanes. Big flying monsters, she had called them. And the notion that she would ever board one? Puh-leeze! At times, the mere thought of attempting such madness would have been enough reason to send her into a mild anxiety attack. But a nerve-racking episode with her mother before a vacation trip to New York City had, strangely enough, turned out to be just the remedy for her fears of flying.

Candace had been just twelve years old at the time, and she had somehow lost track of her mother while they were waiting for their flight to depart. She had become engrossed, naturally, in some novel in one of the magazine shops and when the story had finally ended she looked around and saw that Analee was nowhere to be found. As it had turned out, her mother had gone to check on travel arrangements and had gotten understandably lost inside the colossally spread out Dallas/Fort Worth airport. What a terrible, gut-wrenching nightmare that had been . . . for both of them.

When mother and daughter finally reunited almost two hours later, Candace could genuinely admit that the fear of becoming separated from her mother was much, much greater than the fear of flying on an airplane. Thus the first steps toward conquering her phobia were taken. Over the years, she had grown accustomed to and at better ease with flying—to the point where she now used this method of transportation more frequently than some people drive automobiles.

Now, with her eyes closed and a contented expression adorning her face, she appeared to be just moments from drifting off to sleep. But in reality, her mind was engaged in a multitude of various thoughts—how to strengthen her relationship with her father, her present feelings concerning Tasha's emotional state, and of course—the interview with the man she currently was on her way to meet. The whole nation was talking about this man and already heralding him as one of the great motivational speakers of all time.

More than simply an interview with Jermaine Hill, this was to be a feature story as well. And, as Candace was well aware, all features possessed a hook of some sort—an angle from which the central theme of the story hung. She had been mulling over several angles to employ, but she generally found herself coming back to the same question—who or what motivated the greatest inspirational speaker in the nation? What was *his* source of inspiration?

Her primary goal was to obtain as much personal information as she could (at least, as much as he was willing to share) and then assimilate those juicy tidbits into a literary tour de force that would give his fans exactly what they craved. Jermaine Hill—the story behind the glory.

No, that sounds too cliché . . .

On a scale from one to ten, she supposed her preparation for this story had been a five. A six, maybe. Those projections were unusually low for her since she normally studied her feature subjects with the exacting thoroughness of an operating surgeon. But because this assignment was not an academic or socially instructive article, she hadn't given her lack of research much thought. Simply put, this was a celebrity piece—*"a lot of fluff and cream puff,"* as her mentor, Dr. West, was known to term such works. And though it would provide her with the largest single readership she had ever written for, she still would rather write more serious-minded features. She was content to leave the cheesy fanfare and glitz to the writers who based their merit on style rather than substance.

"Our estimated time of arrival into Los Angeles International Airport is three hours, twenty-eight minutes," the pilot's voice announced. "We are expecting no weather-related interruptions; the temperature in southern California is a pleasant eighty-four degrees."

Eighty-four degrees without the humidity . . . that'll be nice . . . She opened her carry-on case situated at her feet and extracted a leather-bound portfolio notebook. Although her laptop was stowed in the above compartment, her first preference was always the old-fashioned standbys of a pen and loose-leaf sheets of paper. She liked to think it was the intimate, almost sensual, smooth stroke of the pen onto the paper that over the years had become a therapeutic act for her.

"Child, you are forever writing something," Analee had always lightly reprimanded Candace, because her daughter was never without a pen in her hand. But those admonishing words simply had become reverse psychology to the ambitions of her daughter, serving to motivate her even more. Consequently, anything had been fair game for Candace to doodle on at any given time, from napkins and church bulletins to newspapers and blank spaces in her mother's fashion magazines.

Analee had viewed her daughter's writing infatuation as a hobby that she hoped Candace would outgrow. And the sooner, the better. Her maternal reasoning was that there was no career to be had or lifestyle to be lavishly lived as a . . . writer. But after Candace landed a position as a contributing youth columnist for the *Dallas Morning News* in her junior year of high school and then steadily gained acclaim in certain literary circles, Analee was forced to concede that perhaps her daughter's writing was more than a passing hobby.

"Alright, Jermaine Hill," she began, whispering to herself. "What's your real story?" She outlined several introductory questions on her paper by methodically filling in the blank spaces and lines, oblivious to the passing of time as the minutes ticked by. And as the once-blank outline took shape and changed into a more complete synopsis, little by little she began to see how she would conduct the interview. When the plane's wheels touched down on the LAX runway three and a half hours later, her rating on the projection scale was now up to an eight or nine. Whoever this celebrity mystery man was and whatever his source of inspiration, Candace felt newly confident that she would find out all about him.

• • •

STANDING MERE INCHES from the rocky terrain of dirt and vegetation descending from the cliff's edge to the ocean did not seem to be a safe thing to do. But Jermaine had no intention of jumping. At least not yet, anyway. Roughly ten feet behind him was the metal guardrail that fenced in the narrow shoulder of Pacific Coast highway from this very cliff. After another lonely drive to Laguna Beach done for the sole purpose of squandering time between endless photo sessions and talk-show tapings, he had parked along the shoulder and climbed over the guardrail. Now he stood, staring with a morbid sense of admiration at the calm, blue-green body of water almost directly beneath him. The glassy surface of the ocean, casting pools of glimmering pearl-like reflections of sunlight, beckoned ever so seductively to him.

And where would you take me?

Did it matter where the ocean would take him? If nothing else, it would take him away from here, far away from a hypocritical life he was tired of leading. The fans, the shows, the contracts, the pressure . . .

The *pressure.* When Jermaine reduced everything in his life down to a foundation, he swore time and time again that he found this pressure. It ate at him, the pressure from the comparisons to other orators and speakers; from the larger and more ostentatious contracts Mario brokered for him, demanding that the one and only Jermaine Hill be paid top dollar; pressure from the millions of people who placed him on a pedestal, looking to their idol for words of inspiration that might give meaning to their humdrum, dreary lives. Additionally, pressure came from the fickle media, whose coverage was quick to laud him for his positive contributions but quicker still to crucify him alive at the slightest scent of something scandalous.

When he had visualized a career that would afford him success and fame, he had magnified only the glamour of it. He was either naïve enough or ignorant enough to somehow not realize there were negative aspects to such a life. He needn't be reminded of the positives, for he knew those all too well. He knew such a flamboyant lifestyle held power—power that his very pores exuded like a rich cologne the second he entered a room. Power that would cause women to literally throw themselves at him, wanting desperately to have him, if only for one night.

And of course, he knew there was money—ridiculous amounts of money that would continually flow in as a result of his upcoming book deal that was going to shatter every financial record for motivational speakers. And since his show was heard in the top media markets nationwide, he was an advertising magnet for sponsors looking to link their products with the man "guaranteed to get you excited and inspired about life!"

He had known all of this, then had the business sense to link up with the shrewdest, craftiest agent in the business in order to be successful to the point of becoming peerless. One writer for the *Los Angeles Times* had even gone so far as to write a few months earlier that "Jermaine Hill is giving the motivational speaking world the same jolt that Tiger Woods gave the golf world in 1996 upon turning pro."

Jermaine had known and wholeheartedly embraced all of this, pursuing such a life with the zeal of a thirsty man who has glimpsed a mirage of water in the desert. But just as all mirages were false reality, he soon discovered that he had found . . . nothing. After the money and power, after the glamour and fame, there was . . . well there was . . . absolutely nothing. Nothing except for the vast emptiness of the ocean, which was now beckoning to a misplaced fish dying inside of a dried-up fishbowl.

chapter eight

THE WEATHER WAS indeed a pleasant eighty-four degrees as Candace exited the plane and headed into the LAX terminal. After the September 11, 2001, tragedy, the security for airport terminals had become considerably tighter, so the once-normal custom of people's waiting in the terminals for arriving passengers had been abolished. Being alone as she walked to the baggage claim area was nothing new for Candace, however; by now, she was used to traveling by herself, both to conduct interviews and to do needed research for her magazine articles.

What she was *not* accustomed to, however, was the limousine arranged by Mario that picked her up from the airport and transported her to her hotel. A lovely gesture, Candace thought. She certainly didn't mind the pampering, which was all the nicer since she was already feeling a little special about being handpicked for this assignment. Now, relaxing in the backseat of the limo as it cruised along the freeway, she skimmed over Jermaine Hill's itinerary for the next two weeks.

This is simply unbelievable . . .

As best as she could manage when it was in her control, she purposely avoided hectic day-to-day schedules in her own life. She didn't write well when she had a lot on her mind, so her personal credo was to live life easygoing and laid back. Reading Jermaine's frenzied to-do lists was almost enough to give her a headache. Tomorrow, Monday, he was scheduled to make an early-morning appearance at the downtown Hyatt Regency for the National Broadcasters Association breakfast, leaving immediately afterward to speak at a local high school assembly. Then he was scheduled to go to KKTL's studios to tape some promotional spots for next week's broadcasts. He had a few hours' downtime after that before it was time to mix and mingle with potential corporate sponsors in the luxury suites of Dodger Stadium at the game against the Braves.

As she reviewed the itinerary, Candace began to realize that what she should really be concerned about during the next two weeks was not so much which questions to ask Jermaine, but rather how not to let the frenetic scheduling affect her mental ability to put together a high-caliber feature. Though it might just be a celebrity "fluff" piece, the stipulation that she was supposed to go everywhere Jermaine went would undoubtedly make this assignment one of the most challenging she had ever done.

Well, I'm always telling myself I'm up for a challenge . . .

She looked up from the inch-thick itinerary as she felt the limo slowing, then coming to a complete stop in front of The Beverly Hills Hotel. The driver got out and promptly walked around the car to her door.

Known in some circles as "the Pink Palace" because of its bold pink and green color scheme, the Mission-style resort boasted impeccably landscaped grounds surrounding exotic gardens and bungalows, and Candace was duly impressed as she stepped out of the limousine.

"Miss Clark, Mario Jordan is waiting for you in the lobby," the driver said in his thick British accent as he held the door open for her.

"Thank you," she replied, truly wanting to comment that he looked and sounded just like Geoffrey, the wise-cracking butler from the old sitcom *The Fresh Prince of Bel-Air*. Then she thought better of it. The poor guy probably heard that line all the time.

Right away, she observed that The Beverly Hills was the most extravagant hotel she had ever encountered, and she considered herself a well-traveled person. As she stepped inside the grand lobby, she took note of the plush, elegant decor. The room openly displayed an affluence that most people would come nowhere close to attaining in a lifetime. A part of Candace wanted to click her heels together like Dorothy to see if this place was real or if she were dreaming. Her own two-story home in Houston, beautiful and wonderful as it was, paled in comparison.

"Candace Clark, it is an honor and a pleasure to meet you," Mario Jordan announced as he strolled across the foyer to her. Dressed in a tailored Jones New York navy suit and gold tie, he made Candace immediately feel a bit underdressed—she in her travel-comfortable denim blue jeans and white cotton blouse.

"I've read your work for years, and you were the one

person we just had to have to do this interview," he continued, gushing over her as he gently took and shook her hand.

"Thank you. I'm . . . well, flattered. At a loss for words, actually. And that doesn't happen too often," she added with a smile. He smiled back, then quickly glanced down at his watch, immediately creating the impression that he was a man at the mercy of schedules and last-minute deadlines.

"Jermaine should be arriving here shortly and you'll have the rest of the afternoon to get acquainted and go over anything you'd like with him. I trust you've had an opportunity to look over the itinerary already?"

Candace nodded. "Yes, but . . . well, in past interviews I've had some guidelines or boundaries concerning the people I'm covering. And I suppose this is different since I've never covered someone for two weeks, but are there any parameters I need to be aware of?"

"Parameters? No, no—it's like I told Carl Daniels. Candace, this is your story; your baby. Based on your previous work, I know you've got that rare ability to mix professional journalism with some slammin' urban flavor."

Candace couldn't help but smile at Mario's colorful description of her work.

"Nobody else that I've read has the ability to do that. So, I believe you're going to give Jermaine's fans exactly what they want . . ."

Oh, do you, now?

". . . and that, bottom line, it will be a top-quality job." He held out his hands. "So, you've got free rein.

Two weeks to witness him behind the scenes and up close and personal. Now of course I'll have a look at everything before it's sent to *Song of Solomon* to be printed, but I trust your writing instincts and judgment." He raised an eyebrow. "Interesting choice of magazine, though. Any particular reason?"

Candace shrugged, for a moment unsure of how to answer. "Well, let's just say that for this story, I trust *their* instincts and judgment."

"Fair enough. Listen, I do apologize, but I have to run. But here's your room key; your bags have already been taken up. The concierge will give you a call when Jermaine arrives, but knowing him, it'll probably be another half hour or so. One of the things you'll quickly find out about Jermaine is that he doesn't grasp too well the meaning of the word *punctual*."

• • •

THE UPCOMING QUESTION-and-answer game would be typical, Ambrose thought to himself as he wearily plopped down in the chair opposite the psychologist. Twice a week now, they were testing his mind to determine how much progress was being made in his so-called treatment as a mental case. He didn't particularly care to be subjected to these tests, like some sort of caged-up laboratory mouse, but it wasn't as though he really had a choice.

If this is my cross to bear, then so be it, Jesus . . .

By all previous accounts, he believed himself to be a rational man, posing no immediate threat to society. His records were immaculate, not even a single speeding ticket to his name. He had been accused of being mentally unbalanced because of his adamant demand to preach the gospel anywhere he chose. And he was not ignorant; he understood that his right to free speech had been protected under the First Amendment to the Constitution. So what was the problem? Being loud? Getting on someone's nerves with the good news of the gospel?

No, the real problem is the spirit prevailing over Hollywood . . . He knew that you could say and do anything you wanted in this increasingly liberal, immoral society just as long as you didn't speak the name of Jesus.

The enemy, the prince of the power of the air, had a firm stronghold on the movies, television shows, and culture that pervaded Hollywood and affected the rest of the country, even the world. After traveling to various parts of the country, Ambrose had felt the call to come back here and begin attacking the forces of darkness that were subtly leading generation after generation of people into spiritual blindness. A huge task to be sure, but was there anything too hard for the Lord?

"Will you tell me your name and date of birth?" the psychologist began.

Ambrose sighed, wanting to tell this man a whole lot more than just his name and birth.

• • •

NEEDING TO FEEL REFRESHED after she had put most of her garments away, Candace rewarded herself with a quick shower. She would rather have taken a few hours or so to lazily lounge in the tub with some candles lit and Boney James playing sax softly in the background, but time did not allow it. More specifically, her time—soon to become Jermaine Hill's time—did not allow it. She had just finished putting on a beige business-casual pantsuit when the phone rang.

"Hello?"

"Miss Clark, your guest has arrived and is waiting in the lobby. Shall I send Mr. Hill up, or would you rather come down to meet him?"

"Oh, you can send Mr. Hill up, Mr. . . . I'm sorry, what was your name?"

"Pierre, madam. Whatever you need during the next two weeks, it will be my pleasure to personally ensure that those needs are met."

"Why, thank you, Pierre." *Oh, I've died and gone to Heaven . . .*

The knock on her door came several minutes later. Candace checked her appearance one last time in the bathroom mirror, kicking herself mentally as she did so. It was her mother Analee's fault that she could be so vain at times. What did it matter what she looked like? This was strictly a job, a journalistic assignment like the countless others she had done over the years. Then again, she believed this like she believed the good chances of a snowstorm in Houston. This was *not* just another celebrity fluff piece, much as she would have liked to think so. Jermaine Hill was one of the most recognizable voices in America, and the intrigue and star-gazing surrounding him were quickly elevating him to icon status.

"We finally meet," she said as she opened the door. "Jermaine, it's a pleasure." He shook her hand and politely nodded.

"I'm glad to know that." Then flashing a winning smile, he added, "Let's see if you're still saying that line after two weeks with me, though." They both shared a tension-clearing laugh, and Candace stepped aside to let him in.

"Man, this suite is large," he commented as he stepped into the luxurious den area. "Mario told me all your accommodations were being taken care of, and he can sure say that again."

"The Beverly Hills is definitely wonderful," she agreed. "I feel like royalty just walking around this room."

"No doubt." Jermaine took a seat on the plush sofa. "So, Candace, I'm sure you've got a million things you want to ask me."

Candace sat down across from him. "First off, all my friends call me Candi."

"I'm a friend, now?" Again, the winning smile. It was the smile of a person who knows more than probably what should be known. Candace wasn't sure how much of that smile was his public persona or his actual personality. Her mission during the next fourteen days was to clearly know the difference between the two.

"You have a chance to be one," she replied, matching his wit. "At any rate, please feel free to call me Candi."

"Alright. Candi. So, how do you want to go about doing this?" He fidgeted uncomfortably on the sofa. Candace thought she saw some slight hesitation register on his face as he opened his mouth to continue. "If I can be completely honest, though . . . "

Please do . . .

". . . I'm not exactly thrilled with this assignment. Nothing against you, of course, but . . . well, I've seen interviews done in this manner that have taken a drastically opposite turn from how they were intended to go. Mario says you're the best, and going along with him the past couple of years has worked out great for me, but I'd still like to know your angle."

"That's a fair question. Jermaine, truthfully—I don't have a real angle. I guess I'm in that tiny two percent of people who haven't followed your rise to stardom with Elvis-like intensity. My take on this story is going to be strictly objective."

"The impartial juror, is that it?"

"You could say that. I know it sounds odd but my angle for this feature is that, honestly, *I have no angle.* I don't know anything about you. But apparently, there's a mystique surrounding you, because even your most loyal fans don't know much about you, either. So with your help, I'm simply going to give those fans a behind-the-scenes glimpse of their favorite motivational speaker."

• • •

JERMAINE HAD BEEN trying to get a read on this journalist from the second she opened the door. Was she like that pesky, irritating Chantal Dixon from *Star-Watch News*? Or cool, calm, and collected yet looking to pounce on emotional weaknesses like Barbara Walters? Maybe somewhere in between like Oprah? But as she continued to talk, Candi Clark was gradually appearing to be none of the above to him. She had a transparency and innocence that intrigued him as much as it worried him. She was still young, and thus still possessed that youthful thirst for getting all the facts straight, which was of great concern to him. Because with the exception of Mario, he purposely chose not to hang around anyone for any great length of time. It was easier that way to hide his depression, the pills, and the suicidal thoughts that continued to torment him. But even Mario, chaotic as his agent's schedule could be, had lately noticed that something was wrong with Jermaine. Surely, then, his problems could be detected if someone else were to somehow get close to him. And with this young reporter, with no story angle and no real interest in Jermaine other than to give his fans an up-close view of him, it was going to be her single-minded mission to get as close to him as possible.

The truth, Candi? To quote Jack Nicholson, well, she couldn't *handle* the truth. Nobody could—not even himself on any given day.

Quickly running a number of options through his mind, he finally settled on doing the one thing that would ensure his continued control of this interview. As in all interviews, he was under an obligation to give a response to whatever she asked him (within reason, of course). Otherwise she'd see him as being evasive and could convey that to his fans, as good a writer as she was. But he could maintain control if he did this one, simple thing. It was brilliant, really.

"Candi, I'm going to give you the green light to ask me anything you want to. But I have a small stipulation to that."

"I'm listening."

"Whatever you ask me, I'll answer truthfully, to the

best of my knowledge. But only if I have the freedom to ask you the same question."

Candace held up a finger, shaking her head slowly. A small smile played with the curve of her lips. "Oh no, Jermaine. I'm not the one being interviewed here. I don't think that would be a good idea."

"On the contrary—it would be a great idea. Hear me out for a second. Would you agree that the success of an interview could be attributed to the ease and familiarity of the interviewer and interviewee?"

"In many cases, yes. But not always. Sometimes it's better to have complete objectivity."

"I feel you on that. But you should know as well as anybody that there's no such thing as *complete* objectivity in the media. I hate to say it, but media bias is alive and well."

Candace arched an eyebrow. "You're saying you don't trust me?"

"I'm saying the same thing you told me not five minutes ago. I don't *know* you. It's easier to open up to someone if you know you have the same freedom and latitude in conversation that they have."

Candace nodded slowly to herself, her eyes staring into space as if she were lost in deep thought.

"You've made a great point, Jermaine," she finally said after considerable time had passed. "If I didn't know any better, I'd say you were an excellent motivator. Alright, fine, I'll agree to your little stipulation."

Jermaine leaned back on the sofa and resisted a chauvinistic impulse to flash another smile. Yes, he was good at what he did. Scary good. And he had Candace Clark right where he wanted her.

chapter nine

SO, WHAT'S YOUR favorite book?" Candace asked, pressing the record button on her miniature but extremely efficient tape recorder. She also had her pen and notebook on hand—having learned the hard way years before that even the best of tape recorders sometimes break down at the most inopportune times.

"My favorite book?" Jermaine squinted his eyes and rubbed the bottom of his chin. Candace knew she had just thrown him a curve for openers. She was forever asking people this very same question. She loved doing so because the response revealed so much about a person.

"Yes, your favorite book. I'd like to know which book has captured the imagination of the great Jermaine Hill." She figured it wouldn't hurt to play up to the man's ego.

"Fiction or nonfiction?"

"Either."

"Hmm . . ." He rubbed his chin some more. "I'd probably have to say the *Autobiography of Malcolm X.*"

Wow . . . this brother's going deep on me . . . "And why is that?"

"So much history to it, you know? And right at the height of the civil rights movement, too. For Malcolm to experience the childhood that he did, growing up in a time when the definition and worth of a black man was just above that of a dog in some states; for him to learn what he did and then captivate and hold the attention of the world—well, it's . . . it's always been quite the motivating tool for me."

"Do you see yourself now as a twenty-first-century Malcolm X, in the way that you also have seemingly captivated the nation's attention?" *"Almost overnight?"* she thought to herself.

Jermaine immediately shook his head. "No, I wouldn't go there. I'm not serious politically like Malcolm was. My thing is to get people excited and inspired about life, remember?" He flashed his smile again, but this time Candace thought she could see right through it.

You're hiding something, Mr. Hill . . . "Yes, I remem—"

"What's *your* favorite book?"

Both the interruption and the question itself caught her off guard. It was as if he was playing a chess game over who controlled the interview. And she had only asked one question thus far.

"Are you going to do this to me after every question?"

He smiled slowly, almost lazily. "No, not after every question. Only the ones I really want answers to."

Isn't that wonderful . . . She purposely took a considerable amount of time, pretending to be in deep thought. She didn't have to do that, of course. Every writer had a favorite book. Several, in fact. "Well then, in that case I would have to say *The Color Purple.*"

"Why's that?"

"Hey, who's interviewing who, here?"

Jermaine held up his hands. "Thought we had a deal. I'm just asking you the questions you asked me."

"You're right by technicality only—you know that, don't you? Okay, why is it my favorite? Let's see—it deals with complex issues surrounding a woman's coming-of-age, there are rich, colorful characters and dialogue, great Southern history, Alice Walker won the Pulitzer from it—I think you're getting the picture here."

He nodded. "You're painting a pretty clear one." He cleared his throat and with an amused expression added in an oratorial voice, "God gets pissed off if you walk past the color purple in a field and don't see it."

"Very good, Shug Avery. You read the book?"

He shook his head. "Naw. Saw the movie, though. Should've won Best Picture in 1985. Don't know what the Academy was thinking of, giving it to *Out of Africa*. Probably snubbed it because Spielberg was directing it."

"A film buff, huh? Interesting. Well, the Academy Awards are always political; I know a friend of a friend who could tell you some wild stories about that whole process. But back to books, Jermaine, what's the last one you've read?" Another one of her favorite questions. This time, though, there wasn't any hesitation in his response.

"*A Lesson Before Dying.*"

What? "The Ernest Gaines classic?"

"Yeah, that's the one."

It took a few moments for Candace to realize the always-churning gears in her brain had temporarily shut down. She found herself in a little state of shock because of the *what-are-the-chances-of-that* coincidence that the last book she, too, had read was *A Lesson Before Dying.* The Houston Public Library had just implemented a citywide reading push featuring the former National Book Critics Circle award winner, and she had been a guest panelist for one of the local PBS discussions. She had first read the book in high school, but re-reading it had proven to be a great delight for her.

Slowly and hopefully inconspicuously, she took a deep breath. "Why . . . why did you happen to read that?" It was only then that she realized the very real possibility that Jermaine might ask her the name of the last book *she* had read, as well. And the last thing she wanted to do was answer identically.

Stupid little interview stipulation . . . I don't know why I ever agreed to this . . .

To her relief though, Jermaine just shrugged indifferently, as if the question bored him. "I guess I just found the title to be kind of interesting . . ."

• • •

THE OPERATION WAS NOW running smoother than the engine of a well-oiled stock car, although Myra admittedly had some major worries initially.

Would they have the capability and resources to put *Song of Solomon* on every newsstand and bookstore across the country? Could their small staff handle the public relations and advertising blitzkrieg that was inevitably coming? And after years of praying and waiting for a breakthrough opportunity to cross their path, were they in fact prepared and ready now that such a chance had come?

As Myra finished approving the third set of comps to the cover for the next edition, the all-too-true adage of "Be careful what you pray for" stuck in her harried mind like peanut brittle to sore gums. Over the past few days, she had made and answered more phone calls, sent and received more faxes and e-mails, approved more invoices, and signed more operations checks than a high-level manager for a Fortune 500 company. And though she was presently dog-tired, though her ankles last night had swollen to the size of tennis balls, though she hadn't slept more than three hours in the past week, nevertheless she felt an exhilaration in her fulfilled soul that she had never before experienced. For it had been worth it—all the rejecting phone calls she suffered while trying to persuade venture capitalists to invest in her magazine. The "girl you must be crazy" looks she did her best to ignore from her former coworkers as she cleaned out her desk on that last day working for corporate America. The subsequent months of eating Ramen noodles and hot dogs for dinner because the bulk of her money, meager earnings that they were, stubbornly were committed to the financial well-being of the fledgling magazine.

"This magazine is a ministry, and it's bigger than

you," she would remind herself every day as she watched dollar after precious dollar be poured into the initial production setup. Her own personal bills and credit had suffered because she refused to be late or delinquent with anything concerning *Song of Solomon.* She had almost as much love and commitment to it as she had to her only son. For this publication was her child, too. And in many ways, giving birth to her dream had been much, much harder than giving birth to Tyrone.

With a sigh, she slowly stood up from her desk and limped toward her living room. The swelling in her ankles had gone down slightly from yesterday; she would stay off her feet as much as possible for the next several days. *As much as possible*, of course, being the operative words, now that the edition with the Jermaine Hill interview would be ready for distribution in four weeks. One month. Candace Clark would finish the interview in another week and a half and have the story done in time for the July edition of *Song of Solomon*, as per the contract. And for Myra, that was perfect because summer was always the ideal time for peak sales. The magazine industry knew this as much as the book and movie industry did. And while the latest Hollywood talk coming through the grapevine centered on the Fourth of July blockbuster movie featuring Will Smith and the latest model heartthrob, the talk in the equally competitive magazine industry was even more heated over the Jermaine Hill interview. It was much anticipated, that was for sure. And there was buzz about her magazine, with its core mission statement of aiming to publish articles and information of urban societal interest in a manner and spirit that glorified God.

"To You be the glory," Myra breathed as she settled back in her La-Z-Boy recliner. She picked up a large remote control resting on the sofa table beside her and pointed it at her stereo system. Seconds later, the melodious sounds of CeCe Winans's worship-inspiring ballad "Alabaster Box" filled every nook and cranny of the living room. Yes, Myra Washington was tired and her swollen feet hurt, yet her face wore an expression of sheer contentment.

"I'm finally here, Lord. I'm doing Your wonderful will for my life . . ."

It had been during the summer of 1965 when she had asked Jesus Christ to be the Savior and Lord over her life. At just seven years old, she certainly had not grasped the full extent as to what such a prayer truly meant. Nevertheless, she believed that God had something special in store for her life. And as her Uncle Po weekly taught the Sunday school lessons to her in an easy, uncomplicated manner, her knowledge of God's Word and will for her life grew each year.

Later, when she'd left tiny Macon for the big city of Atlanta to attend Spelman College, her Uncle Po had faithfully written her weekly devotionals to help her stay focused. She'd kept those letters and even now, after all this time, she still occasionally pulled them from her desk to re-read them.

As CeCe Winans continued to sing about the symbolic cost of oil in her alabaster box, Myra couldn't help but sing right along, albeit off-key. Not that such a trivial issue mattered. Who cared if she couldn't sing like CeCe?

I paid a high price to get here . . . Lord knows I'm now going to enjoy every minute of it . . .

• • •

"CANDI! GIRL, YOU are starring in my dream! Living in Hollywood with that fine-looking Jermaine Hill, spending—"

"I am *not* living with the man," Candace corrected her friend over the phone, wondering once more why that crucial fact was not registering in Tasha's brain.

"Yeah, girl. Whatever. So you met him already, huh? Spill it, sis. Give your girl some details."

As Candace stretched out on the luxurious recliner, she was torn between telling Tasha the truth or what the poor girl wanted to hear.

How 'bout this, Tasha—the man's built like a bodybuilder and last night we fed each other chocolate-covered strawberries in his private Jacuzzi . . .

"Well, he's nice, I guess. Tall. He smells good, too. I can't place that particular cologne right off, but—"

"Well then, ask him what he wears! I mean, you're supposed to be interviewing him, right?"

"Yes."

"Good! Girl, go on."

"What else do you want me to say? We talked about his favorite books, foods, colors, sports teams—just surface information for right now. I didn't want to overwhelm the guy on the first day."

"Good thinking. Keep it simple at first, then go in for the kill."

"Tasha, this is a simple celebrity interview. No kills or anything like that. I really don't see why everybody goes crazy over him in the first place."

"Oh, come on! You mean to tell me that when you're looking at him, you don't just wanna rip his clothes off and—"

"Tasha!"

"I'm just saying, girl. Anyway, if you don't care for him, you're still gonna hook me up, right?"

Candace sighed. "What, exactly, was it you wanted me to do again?"

"Slip him my number and picture, Candi! And not that one from college where my thighs are showing those few extra pounds. Give him the one we took when we went to South Padre Island. After putting in four months at the gym, I was looking real sexy."

"Tasha . . ."

"C'mon Candi . . . I'd do the same for you."

No you wouldn't . . . because I'd never stoop so low as to do something like this . . .

"So, you gonna hook me up?"

"Yeah, Tasha. I got you." *And I'm praying for you, too . . .*

chapter ten

THE SCRAPBOOK BULGED, overflowing with countless faded and yellowing pictures that did not fit into the plastic sleeves. The book itself was extremely dog-eared, but that didn't concern Bell much. Because to her feeble mind, these pictures were one of the last things she could hold on to. And even her grip on these was tenuous.

Sadly, she didn't remember most of the people in the old photographs anymore, scores of people who were hugging her, laughing with her, crying with her. Who *were* all these people who had touched her life, even if only for a moment? It had taken almost seventy years and a crippling mental disease to remind her that the sum total of life equaled nothing but memories. And what was she to do as those memories slowly diminished, like flower petals leaving the protective, nurturing stem in a gusty breeze?

Oh, Jesus . . . oh sweet Jesus . . . I'll never forget you . . .

One solitary picture, like that airborne rose petal, fell to the floor at her feet. With an effort, she reached down with trembling fingers and retrieved it. Turning it over, she saw the smiling, confident face of her Jermaine on his high school graduation day.

Such a handsome, handsome man . . . you made your mama proud that day . . .

That boy had grown up much too fast. He'd almost had to, given the tumultuous conditions of his early childhood. Bell had done all she could to help, though seemingly all the love she had poured into him wasn't making much of a difference.

Train up a child in the way he should go . . .

She had done that, though. Lord knows, she had done that. So it was in her Father's hands now.

Save my son, Jesus . . .

• • •

"TELL ME ABOUT your childhood, Jermaine," Candace asked. "Your parents, your friends . . . your life growing up. What were some of the good things you remember?" A sly grin crossed her face as she added, "and while you're at it, you can throw in a couple of bad things, too."

She would have preferred riding like royalty again in the limousine, but Jermaine insisted on driving his Escalade everywhere he went. This drove Mario crazy because his client was almost always late for his appointments, but Jermaine was as stubborn as a blind mule with bad legs on that issue. He maintained that it was the one little bit of freedom and privacy he still had.

"There's not much to tell."

"Then tell me what little of it there is to tell," she

quickly replied. No way was he going to get out of that one so easily.

"Alright. Well, I was born in Brooklyn, right there off Twenty-third and Stillwell. Don't remember much about New York, though, because I was outta there by the time I was three years old. My parents—Shirley and Jermaine Hill Sr. . . . they, well . . ." As his words trailed off, he shook his head in what Candace thought might be disgust.

"Those people hit that crack pipe so much and so hard that when they weren't raising hell in the 'hood trying to score that next hit, they were somewhere on the street passed out. Child Services was threatening to come take me, so my mom's oldest sister, Bell, came and got me. Took me to Baltimore to live with her."

"Did you ever go back to live with your parents?"

Jermaine shook his head. "Naw. My pops was killed in a drug deal gone bad two years after I left. Then, my mom got arrested after robbing a convenience store. Pleaded guilty to armed robbery, but it was her third strike so she got sent upstate to Bedford Hills." He shook his head again. "She died six months after that. The doctors said she had a bad heart. She was like a time bomb for years and didn't even know it."

With a sensitivity and empathy Candace didn't even know she had inside her, she automatically reached out and lightly put her hand on Jermaine's arm.

"I'm so sorry, Jermaine."

"Thanks," Jermaine replied. "She died on Thanksgiving Day, 1977. I remember the exact date 'cause we got the call from the hospital during halftime of the Cowboys-Lions game. But it wasn't hard on me, though.

I was just a kid, y'know? And I didn't remember my moms or my pops that well, anyway. To me, they were a couple of addicts who just happened to give birth to me. Her death was harder on Aunt Bell. To this day, that old woman breaks down and cries like a baby whenever someone talks about her Shirley." He bit down on his lower lip and Candace supposed he was fighting hard to not reveal much emotion on this obviously sensitive subject. "She's one of the few people that old woman even remembers anymore."

That old woman? "Jermaine, are . . . are you close to her? Your Aunt Bell, I mean. She was the one who really raised you and all."

Jermaine turned and looked at her. "I'll answer that after you first tell me a little about your family. Some good things and, while you're at it, some of the bad things, too." He smiled broadly.

What? "Jermaine, I . . . I had a flow going here. You're messing up the rhythm when you start asking me questions out of the blue like that. We . . . we were talking about your Aunt Bell."

"No, it was *me* doing all the talking about that old woman. And that's cool. It's just that now, it's your turn to talk about your past."

I cannot believe I agreed to this . . . if Dr. West could see me now . . . Candace took a long, deep breath and closed her eyes, thinking for the umpteenth time since yesterday how this was definitely going to be her most challenging assignment to date. But she refused to stress over Jermaine's little interview-stipulation game. She would play along, if only to get the prized information she needed for this story.

"I'm an only child, Jermaine, if you must know. I was born and raised in Dallas, although I traveled a lot all throughout my childhood. That was mostly to please my mother, though. All she ever wanted was for her little girl to see the world." Predictably, she felt a tightness in her throat at the sudden remembrance of Analee, and she sensed her eyes beginning to get all moist. Quickly, she blinked away what would have been potentially embarrassing tears.

"I take it you and your mom are close, then?"

"Yes. Well . . . yeah. You could say that, I suppose. We, ah . . . actually we *were* close. Very close. She passed away six years ago from . . . from breast cancer." *God, did I just say that?*

Candace was both surprised and a tad horrified that she was revealing so much personal information. What shocked her the most was how *easy* it seemed to be to open up around Jermaine. And she wasn't sure why. More than likely it was because she could sense and furthermore relate to his obvious pain of not having many people to hold a conversation with. She was in the same boat, and she knew it. Aside from Tasha (who definitely danced to the bizarre beat of her own music), Candace rarely was in an environment or a social setting where she could freely open up and simply be herself. Partly, that was her fault—she had somehow developed tunnel vision on her quest to win a Pulitzer and several relationships had been hurt along the way. Including a major falling-out with a man she had wrongly and misguidedly thought was *the* one . . .

"Sorry to hear about that," Jermaine offered, interrupting her wandering thoughts with his rich baritone voice. He really did have a nice voice, she had to admit. "And I can tell it was hard on you since you two were so close."

Candace nodded. "After she died, I had a lot of questions. I kept them inside because nobody was really there to answer them. Above all, I couldn't understand why God took my mother like that. It . . . wasn't fair."

"I know what you mean."

"Do you believe in God, Jermaine?" She hadn't even meant to ask him such a question; the opportunity just presented itself.

Jermaine shrugged. "Hard to say, sometimes."

"What's so hard to say about it? Either you do or you don't, right?"

"I was brought up to believe that way, I can tell you that. My Aunt Bell dragged me kickin' and screamin' to church about four times a week. Real hard-core religion, y'know what I'm saying? 'Don't-do-this, don't-do-that.'" He shrugged again. "I guess it didn't rub off on me the way it did her. Don't get me wrong—I believe in God as a higher power. Anyone can look around the world and see things in nature and science that you know a human simply couldn't do."

"Well, do you pray to . . . *whomever* you believe to be that higher power?"

"Sometimes. But it's probably more me talking to myself out loud than to anyone else." He glanced over at her. "How 'bout you? You into God and prayer and all that?"

"I wouldn't say I'm *into* God and prayer as if I attended church every Sunday and said my prayers every night. I remember going to church when I was younger. Both my parents were Christians and my father was even a preacher's son. Every now and then, I'll find myself saying a prayer if I'm facing a difficult issue in my life. I do have faith and I believe God is there, Jermaine. I'm just not so sure He's always listening to what I might have to say."

They were at the Hyatt Regency now, and Jermaine turned off Seventh Street into the parking area where a tuxedoed valet was waiting for them.

"So, you're ready for your big speech?" Candace asked, a bit relieved for the opportunity to change the subject.

He shrugged with a condescending air of nonchalance. "It's not that big a speech. It's just twenty minutes . . . twenty awesome minutes from the man guaranteed to excite and inspire you about life!" he imitated in his best public-address voice.

"Not bad, Jermaine. But I have to tell you, you sound like the kind of guy who always believes his own press."

He quickly shook his head. "Now there's where you're wrong. I never even read anything written about me." He opened his door to get out.

"Not even my article when I finish?"

"Maybe." Looking back over his shoulder he added, "If it's any good."

• • •

THE PACING BACK AND FORTH in his small room was now practically legendary; it was rumored that Ambrose walked ten miles a day without ever leaving his assigned cell. As he paced, he would quote scriptures from the Bible. Spew them from his mouth, in fact, often with the fervor and frantic speed of a used-car auctioneer.

"Yea though I walk through the valley of the shadow of death, I will fear no evil, for thou art with me, thy rod and staff they comfort me . . ." Ambrose was now in the throes of quoting the book of Psalms from memory. Not a specific one or two psalms, but the *entire* book. Normally it would take him a few days to recite it, but he was feeling especially energetic at the moment, and he might exhaust all 150 psalms by sundown. The words were coming from his mouth at such a rapid pace that the sounds were almost unintelligible.

"Surely goodness and mercy shall follow me all the days of my life and I will dwell in the house of the Lord forever . . ."

Presently, nobody was around to tell Ambrose to shut up—it was too early and the old preacher was doing a good job of staying relatively quiet. So on he went, then, through the book of Psalms. Slowly but surely, he was waging war against the enemy.

• • •

"TELL ME WHAT YOU got already," Chantal requested into her hands-free car phone as she navigated through the brisk early-morning traffic on the East L.A. Interchange. With one hand she held a cup of steaming hazelnut-flavored coffee and with the other hand she applied a fresh layer of lipstick, somehow steering the car at the same time. She was talking to a source known to her only as "Spike," a man of many talents who over the years had helped her find the dirt on everybody who was anybody in this town.

"Here's what I got, baby. Candace flew in yesterday afternoon—she was picked up by a limo and is staying at a high-end suite at The Beverly Hills."

"Yeah, yeah, Spike. That's old news. What about her and Jermaine?"

"Calm down, I'm getting to that. You know I'm always going to have the juicy stuff. Jermaine rolled up to her suite yesterday at just past five o'clock, then didn't leave until almost midnight. That's seven hours of so-called just getting to know this girl. And they stayed in the room the whole time. They ordered in room service."

"What did they have?"

"I don't know. Don't have the details on that."

"Spike!"

"What? Even the best sometimes have their limits, baby. But you're missing the point anyway—he picks up Candace this morning at six-thirty, and they just pulled into the downtown Hyatt for the Broadcasters Association breakfast. Listen, this guy's already been with her for almost nine hours—there's definitely something going on here behind the scenes. Ol' Spike can smell it."

"I *knew* it!" Chantal exclaimed, narrowly missing sideswiping a late-model Mercedes in the lane to her right as she punched the air with her fist. "I knew Mario had to have a better reason for using that no-celebrity-story-writing bimbo to do this feature. Jermaine must have a thing with her. Maybe they got some history or something."

"That's what it's looking like to me."

"Spike, can you get me some real good pics on this? I'm working on putting some things together but I'm going to need some nice black-and-whites of our two lovers Jermaine and Candace together. And you know what types of pics I'm talking about."

"Ain't gon' be a problem at all. Your boy Spike is representin'. Don't I always come through for you?" He paused a second before continuing, "and, uh . . . that's cause *you* always come through for me, right?" He started laughing—a lascivious, wicked little laugh.

"You naughty old man," Chantal replied in her best *come hither* voice. Spike was so, so good at a great many other things besides being her best source. "You let me take care of that part of our deal, alright? You just make sure I get those pics before *Song of Solomon* is ready to publish this story."

In her own inflated, self-absorbed world, Chantal often considered herself a good celebrity writer. A great one, even. And the story she was cooking up now on Jermaine Hill was going to make little Miss Candace Clark's boring piece look like a grade school book report by the time she was finished with this whole affair. And not that she meant to be overly spiteful or vengeful, but Mario Jordan had brought this on himself. For he had repeatedly spurned all her requests for one, *just one*, interview with Jermaine. But this new girl Candace, who had never done a celebrity piece before, got to spend two weeks with the man? That was bull, and she knew it. But if that's how they wanted this thing to go down, then so be it.

School was definitely in session, and the Chantal Dixon payback clinic was about to commence wreckin' shop and takin' names.

chapter eleven

THE FIRST FOUR DAYS of the interview went by in a blur for Candace—she was bouncing all over Orange County and the surrounding areas so much that she felt like she was taking a never-ending taxi ride. But at least she was getting her information. Jermaine, remarkably, was opening up to her as freely and comfortably as he'd likely ever opened up to a media representative. Of course, she was having to reveal more about herself than she would have liked. It had been a little awkward at first, this little interview-stipulation game, but her once-blasé attitude about him had begun to soften a bit. She was starting to experience that writer's intuition—the feeling whereby she knew she was going to blow readers away with what she was about to write.

"So why isn't the great Jermaine Hill married?" she asked him as they casually strolled, tourist-like, around Disneyland's Adventureland. Jermaine had come out to the theme park earlier as a celebrity host for part of a media event spotlighting an upcoming movie. Afterward he had some free time, and Candace had never been to Disneyland, so here they were. Employees for the Aladdin's Oasis extravaganza now milled around them like busy worker ants, hurriedly preparing for that afternoon's show. They didn't seem to care that the most famous motivational speaker in America was walking right next to them, probably because they saw and dealt with celebrities every day.

"*Should* I be married?"

"Well, it's a question I'm sure some of your fans would like to know the answer to. Your *female* fans only, I hope." She laughed. "So how about it, huh? You're what, thirty, thirty-one years old? And you've never thought about it?"

He rubbed his chin. Candace noted to herself that he rubbed his chin every time she asked him a hard question. It gave him a little time to think, she supposed.

"Yeah, I've thought about it. But in this town, getting hitched is a joke, y'know? People spend all this money on some lavish ceremony, only to have this nasty split a year later and end up wasting even more money on the settlements. On top of that, you've got the tabloid news crews invading your privacy every time you turn around." He shook his head disgustedly. "I don't know if it's worth all the trouble."

"That's your only reason? The Hollywood culture and tabloids? Come on, I don't buy that. I think the real reason is because you haven't met anyone who connects with you on every level."

Jermaine opened his mouth as if to say something, then shrugged it off.

"What? You were going to say something?" Candace pressed.

"You don't miss a thing, do you? I wasn't going to say anything, just that . . . just that I don't know if that happens anymore."

"If *what* happens anymore?"

"Stuff like finding someone to connect with on every level, y'know? Soul mates, love-at-first-sight kind of thing. I think people get married nowadays more out of convenience than out of love."

"That's an interesting thing to say. You came out of left field with that one. I would have thought a motivator and person of inspiration like yourself would be a true believer in love."

"I'm not saying I don't believe in love—I'm just saying that people don't always get married these days because they fall in love. And if they do, if you look at the current divorce rates, they're obviously falling as quickly *out* of love. But let's go back to love and relationships. And let's take you, for example."

"What about me?" Interview-stipulation game or not, this was one area she preferred to keep under private lock and key, no matter how much her attitude concerning him had warmed.

"Oh, come on. You knew I was going to ask you the same questions you put to me, right? And I don't see a ring on your finger—so the reason you're not married is because you haven't found your soul mate yet? No knight in shining armor? No Prince Charming coming to—"

"You've made your point!" she quickly, and a bit sharply, interjected.

"Want to tell me about it?"

"Tell you about what?"

Chuckling, he continued. "It's not as easy to hide as you may think. Those 'been hurt by a man before' signs are written all over you. You know, I dealt with issues like that on one of my shows a couple of months ago—talking about how we put up walls whenever people hurt us and how that prevents us from loving again." He looked over at Candace imploringly. "I'm a good listener, y'know?"

"No doubt you are. But let's shift those listening ears of yours and get back to you being a good *talker*. I'm working on a deadline here, remember?" She had no desire whatsoever to talk about her past failed stabs at love—all the men she had ever dated had followed the same, tired pattern. As soon as the brotha realized Candace would probably always make more money and enjoy greater levels of success than he, the relationship inevitably went south faster than a flock of geese headed for Florida for the winter. Men and their tired, tired egos . . .

"I know, but we've got us a little rhythm going here," Jermaine replied, smiling. "And I'm sure my fans would, as you say, love to find out about my past relationships." He started grinning slowly, lazily. Then he licked his lips, LL Cool J–style. "I'd be *more* than happy to tell all. After the lady, of course."

Oh, no you don't . . . I'm not ready to open up about that . . . . "Let's switch subjects, Jermaine. We'll come back to relationships later."

Jermaine nonchalantly shrugged his shoulders as if to say, "It's your story."

• • •

AND INDEED IT WAS her story, in his view. But there was a twist. Candace may have been asking all the right questions to find out about him, but only if she played along with the little discovery process he was engaging in too. And not only was he partaking in it, but he was also indirectly controlling the extent of what was said.

Over the past two years, there was always one main version of himself he paraded before the masses—the man with the golden voice, blah, blah, and all that jazz. But unbeknownst to everyone there was another side to him; one that no one had been able to discover. Smiles on the outside, suicidal tendencies on the inside. How could the most recognized voice in the country also hold the most unrecognizable hurt, pain, and loneliness in the country?

Admittedly, it was not his desire to forever carry his dark secrets within him. He didn't want to go to the grave with no one ever knowing of the grossly contradictory, almost schizophrenic, life he had led. But neither was he going to freely offer such damaging information without something in return. And what would be the price for such knowledge? A secret told for a secret given. That something in return had just become the skeletons in Candace Clark's closet. He knew she had some.

Everybody's got some . . .

chapter twelve

ALRIGHT, EVERYBODY, LISTEN UP—yours truly is coming to you with yet another OD of inspiration for your soul," Jermaine began. "My theme for today is freedom. Now there's a lot of ways I can come to you with this, but I'm mainly going to focus on self freedom. Your ability to open up and be uninhibited to live life carefree. To love unconditionally. To be sensually aware of a vibrant world that is all around you. How can you do this? Let Jermaine give you some simple suggestions . . ."

Candace observed carefully from behind the glass partition in the studio, slightly in awe at Jermaine's ability to somehow transform into a different person whenever he was behind the microphone. It was as if he believed, as if he *knew*, that he was the only person who could motivate and inspire his audience. She had noticed this all week for not only his radio show, but also for his every public-speaking event. She likened it to the alter-ego phenomenon of Clark Kent versus Superman. When the spotlight was not focused directly on him Jermaine was sort of a Clark, minus the glasses and clumsy bumbling behavior, of course. But when it was his time to excite and inspire the masses about life, a transcendent confidence and almost supernatural aura came over him. He became Superman—brilliantly reaching and superbly connecting with his audience.

"He's something to watch in person, *sí*?" Vic, KKTL's station manager, commented as he came into the room and sat beside Candace.

"My thoughts exactly."

Vic now turned and faced her. "I can't help but notice that you have a great opportunity to get to know Jermaine with this interview. He, ah . . . he hasn't let you know of his plans once the year is out, has he?"

"No, he hasn't. Why do you ask?" From her first meeting with Vic, she had found the man painfully nervous. She knew exactly what piece of information he was trying to extract from her, but she was going to force him to be more direct.

"Oh, no reason. No reason. But ah . . . *por favor*, you wouldn't happen to know if he has a deal somewhere else?"

"No, I wouldn't. And I would guess that business is strictly between Jermaine and Mario Jordan."

"*Claro que si*. Oh, I'm sorry, *perdona* me—I'm doing it again," he said, his face turning a light crimson. "I sometimes slip back and forth between English and my native tongue."

Yes, especially when you're nervous . . . "Oh, that's alright." She looked at him and offered an understanding smile. "*Yo comprende*. I understand a little Spanish. I live in Houston, remember?"

"Yes, yes," he replied, his face still red. "And you are

right—that information is between Jermaine and his agent." He was silent for a few minutes as they both listened to Jermaine give wonderful insight on how to have self freedom. "But, as you can see, KKTL has been very good to him. And remains good to him. So . . . maybe when you ask him your questions, you can ask about his future plans, *sí*?"

"Yes, I suppose I could ask him."

"*Muchas gracias, muchas gracias!* And . . . and you can perhaps tell me then . . . what those plans are?"

Candace didn't want Vic to have to resort to begging. It wasn't becoming for a person in his management position, she thought. And she could understand his frustration. In all likelihood, he was about to lose his star player and the signature voice of the radio station. Anyone could see that coming.

"Oh, I don't know about that, Vic. I can't divulge anything until the article's in print. I guess you're just going to have to read it when the story comes out like everyone else."

Vic mumbled something sarcastic in Spanish, not realizing that Candace understood every word.

• • •

"GREAT SHOW, JERMAINE. But then, it's always a great show when you're behind the mic, isn't it? I mean, has there ever been a time when you flat-out bombed?" Candace's question prompted a strange look from Jermaine, like she'd just said something blasphemous.

"I'm serious," she continued, "has there ever been a

time when you felt you didn't connect with your audience as well as you would have liked to?"

"Nope. The great Jermaine Hill always—"

"Oh, come on!"

Giving in rather easily to her almost girlish pleading, he shrugged his shoulders as he merged into the traffic headed north on Interstate 5. "Well yeah, I guess there's been a few forgettable times."

"Do tell."

"Alright, but for the record, I plan on hearing a couple of yours, too. Let me think, I guess it was my junior year at Howard. I was on tap to speak at this meeting at some fancy pad in Georgetown. Many major political players were going to be there talking about welfare reform, affirmative action—pretty heavy stuff, y'know? Anyway, I was supposed to speak for about five to ten minutes on how those issues impacted young adults."

"Just five to ten minutes? That seems like a short time for those kinds of issues."

"It wasn't like I was running for office or anything. They already had some members from the Congressional Black Caucus scheduled to speak. I was just filler for the program."

"The voice everybody wanted to hear."

"Yep. The golden voice himself. Can't tell you how much play I was getting with that line back in those days. Anyway, I was pretty hyped up about the chance to rub shoulders with these D.C. elite. So I get to the place, looking all *GQ*." He paused to grandly tug on the lapels of an imaginary tuxedo. "I've got my speech all memorized, made all the mental notes of the people there, even know how I'm gonna drop their names during my speech. Couldn't have been more ready."

"So what happened?"

"Well, I get there and I'm working the crowd like a pro. Networking, shaking the right hands and all that. I find myself next to some businessmen about to propose a toast to a long-standing political science professor at the university. The guy was like a modern-day Booker T. Washington, y'know what I'm saying? I'm near their circle, and I can mingle with the best of 'em, and I happen to overhear one of the men making a big deal out of the wine being a classic 1947 Bordeaux. I didn't drink a lot, but I acted like I did and took the bottle off the tray to admire it. I take a glance at the label, tilting it up so I can see it, and . . . "

"Oh, no . . . don't tell me . . . surely it didn't . . ."

"It did. To this day I don't know how, but the blasted thing spilled all over my white dress shirt and the white lapels on my designer black tux."

"Red wine?" She couldn't hold in her laughter now. "Jermaine, how aawwwful! And . . . and that kind of stain won't come out!"

"Wasn't the worst of it, either. They called my name to go up to the podium not five minutes later. I didn't have time to change, so I had to address the whole room in my stained shirt and coat. And instead of them listening to my voice and what I had to say, all eyes were on the idiot who couldn't keep his shirt clean. Embarrassing like you wouldn't believe. But you know what? After I got over the humiliation of the whole thing, I saw that it actually helped people remember who I was. Right now, you can still walk up to some Congressmen in D.C. and they'll remember me first as the guy who spilled the wine and then only second as some motivational speaker."

"Because it was so funny?" she asked, still laughing.

"Because that was such an expensive bottle. I learned my lesson, though."

"And what was that?"

"Always bring a change of clothes to public functions." He smiled. "No, the real lesson was that sometimes . . . sometimes, it's best to be heard and not seen."

"That's an interesting twist; usually that saying goes the other way. Is that why you like radio broadcasting so much? Because people can simply focus on your voice? And they can't see you?"

He shrugged. "Could be." After driving in silence for a mile or two, he glanced over at Candace. "It's your turn now, by the way."

"My *turn*?"

"Tell me about a time when you wrote something that people thought stunk. And I mean was awful—just unbelievably 'should've never been written, L.A. Clippers' awful."

"Hey, the Clippers aren't that awful."

"They are, too. And don't try to sidestep the question."

"I wouldn't think of it." She turned her gaze toward the window for a moment, causing Jermaine to think that she was definitely stalling. "It's just that . . . well, I honestly don't recall a time when I wrote something people thought was bad."

"Come on, Candi. You expect me to believe that?" *You still can't fully open up, can you?*

"I'm not sure what I expect you to believe, but it's the truth anyway. I mean, you're talking to a girl who was writing for the *Dallas Morning News* at fourteen years old."

"And you never had any critics? Everyone *always* loved your work?"

"Would I sound conceited if I said they did?"

Yeah . . . stuck up, too . . . "Then what about yourself? You telling me you've always been satisfied with the things you write? That you've never thought you could do a better job?"

Candace continued to gaze out the window. "There's always room for improvement, sure. And I'm my own harshest critic when it comes to second guessing. I'm always thinking that I either should have added something or had something taken out from a piece—that I could have somehow made the article better."

Jermaine shook his head. "Answered just like a seasoned politician up for reelection. A lot of gravy, but no meat."

She turned from the window to look at him. "Well, I'm sorry, Jermaine, but I honestly don't recall ever bombing. I've never . . . um, I've never had a wine-on-my-shirt experience when dealing with my writing. At least not one that everybody could see," she added, smiling.

"So you always write winners?"

"Afraid so."

"So this story, this all-inclusive interview with me—you're saying this is definitely gonna be good?"

"Uh-huh. Like they say, it's going to be off the, off the . . . what's that line?"

"Off the hook."

"Yes. Off the hook."

chapter thirteen

THEIR SURVEILLANCE METHODS were borderline illegal, but Chantal's justification was they only resorted to them when needed. Compared with the high-tech spying strategies glorified in cat-and-mouse chase scenes in the movies, the tactics she and Spike used weren't that complex anyway. They didn't have to be—she had learned over the years that when dealing with Hollywood schedules, it paid to have skills with the Rolodex. She had connections throughout the entire industry who could tell her where and when every A-list celebrity was slated to make a public appearance.

Jermaine Hill had been harder to tail than most stars, but her man Spike was very good. And very discreet. He was loyal and knew how to keep his mouth shut. That was his best asset as far as Chantal was concerned, because it wasn't enough for your source to find damaging information on someone if he then just auctioned it off to the highest bidder. She didn't have to worry about that with Spike, though—he worked solely for Chantal. Theirs . . . was a quite mutual and *pleasurable* agreement.

"Got some good news," Spike relayed over the phone to her.

"That's just what I need to hear right now," she said, putting down her third cup of coffee so far that day. "I've had a morning you wouldn't believe." She swiveled away from a computer screen at which she had just spent an unsuccessful three hours trying to get private dirt on who was checking into the Betty Ford clinic. "So what do you have?"

"It's about our two lovers, and it's a gold mine. You know that this upcoming weekend Jermaine's speaking at the United Entertainers banquet in Phoenix, right? Well, the public itinerary has him arriving late Friday night, staying at the Marriott, and speaking at the banquet Saturday afternoon. Get this, though—that same itinerary has him leaving Saturday evening when it's over, but I'm hearing through the grapevine that lover boy is actually not leaving Arizona until Monday morning."

"Monday morning? Why's he staying there two extra days?"

"That's what I wanted to know. So I did some more digging and found out he's secretly going to be holed up at the Phoenician resort in Scottsdale. It's quiet, secluded, romantic, did I mention quiet? Lover boy's booked just *one* room there for him, and you know that Candace Clark is supposed to be everywhere he is for these two weeks."

Chantal bristled. "Don't remind me."

"Right. Anyway, I called in a couple of favors, pulled

a few strings, and got a room booked right across the hall from where they're going to be staying, with access to the adjoining suite."

"Your info is all hush-hush, right? And there's no way to trace it back to us in case people start asking?"

"Chantal, c'mon now. That's almost insulting. You're talking to the best of the best."

She punched the air with her fist. "Yes! This is better than I even thought! Yes . . . yes . . . yes! Sweet mother of . . ." A glorious wave of euphoria washed over her like an incoming Bay Area ocean tide. How sweet this was! Who said hard work didn't pay off? Not only had she worked hard and paid her dues, but she was now sitting on the biggest scandal since . . . well, since . . .

"Spike, you know how the media jumped all over Clinton a few years ago with that Lewinsky mess? Front page of the *New York Times* every day and all that?"

"Yeah."

"And how it was my fantasy to feel that rush Kenneth Starr must have felt to have all the money and resources to hunt down the biggest personality in the country?"

"Yeah." Spike started laughing.

"Well, ol' Mr. Starr might'a had more money, but he didn't get his man." She clucked her teeth together in playful scorn. "Such a waste. But me? Not going to happen. Tell me how that line goes?"

"Chantal Dixon delivers," he answered. "Always."

She punched the air with her fist again, now feeling an adrenaline rush that three cups of coffee came nowhere close to competing with.

• • •

THIS WAS WHERE AND when he liked it most—on his balcony, leaning against the railing of his wooden deck, Duke Ellington's band making melody on his stereo, and an ice-cold glass of strawberry lemonade chillin' in his hand. All the while he was visually taking in the scenic, almost surreal Hollywood Hills landscape. To say it was beautiful would be like saying Michelangelo could paint a lil' bit. The view was absolutely breathtaking. In addition, the stillness of the Pacific coastal air provided a tranquil respite for Jermaine, granting him the one place where he could remove his public mask and simply be himself. Where he could simply be that little kid once again, that confused little kid who couldn't understand why Shirley and Jermaine Sr. didn't love him enough to throw away the crack pipe and leave the street life alone. That kid growing up with a thousand questions that all the grown-ups were too busy to answer. That kid who thought that having unlimited fame and riches was the eternal answer to happiness. Because wasn't that the American dream? Life, liberty, and the pursuit of happiness?

While preparing for a career that involved motivating others, he had read more than his share of the best-selling books full of inspirational quotes, anecdotes, and conversational pieces. He had gotten the bulk of his initial material from speakers and writers like John Maxwell, Les Brown, Zig Ziglar, and T. D. Jakes. And from those interesting and established minds he had developed a style that was all his own. A mix of common sense, urban flavor, and honey-do-right that the country was eating up like sizzling hotcakes. Success had come easy and fast for him; however, one of those speakers years ago had written something that continued to linger in his mind. It haunted his mind, actually.

"Success isn't success without a successor, nor is it success without someone to share it with . . ."

He was currently the most recognized voice of inspiration in the country, but he would give away all that fame and clout just to have Ronny and Eric back in his life. Or just to have someone, anyone in his life who could understand and appreciate him for who he really was. Forget all that "man with the golden voice" marketing machine mumbo-jumbo; the persona created by that spin-doctoring think tank. That line of bull had gone out to people so much and so often that even Jermaine sometimes believed it.

"Success isn't success without someone to share it with . . ."

So maybe a woman was what he needed.

Been there, done that . . .

He wasn't lacking in the dating department, though even now he was slowly admitting to himself that getting into a girl's *bed* and getting inside a girl's *head* were two different challenges. Granted, his fame could knock that first challenge out every single night if he wanted it, but he was tiring of that game. The Hollywood women always fit in the same shallow categories—the wannabes and the has-beens. Either you were hot or you weren't. The classy ladies and divas who were firmly entrenched on the A-list weren't giving it up unless you represented like a gentleman. Sidney Poitier–like.

Let it go . . . who am I tryin' to fool?

The real reason Jermaine wasn't in a close relationship was because he wasn't about to let anyone catch a glimpse of his scarred soul. He knew the closer you got to a person, the more clearly you could see not only the good, but the bad and ugly as well. And though the world chose to exclusively see him through the rose-colored glasses of celebrity, he also knew this golden-voiced speaker had some bad and ugly qualities simmering just beneath the surface.

Those dark blotches were slowly taking him out, and he knew it. But for the most part, he didn't care. Why should he? It wasn't like anybody else cared either. He wasn't hearing *"Jermaine, how are you doing today? What's on your mind?"* or *"If you need to talk, I'm here to listen"* from people during the course of his day or week. No, people only came to him to hear what *he* had to say for them. To make inquiries as to what he could do for them. Motivate me, Jermaine. Inspire me, man! Make me feel . . . alive!

Make them feel alive. Yeah, he could do that alright. This thing called "life" was a crazy thing, though. Because the more he made the public feel alive, the more a large part of him wanted to do exactly the opposite. The two states of existence—life and death—were more closely linked than most ignorant people realized. But Jermaine didn't fit into that category of ignorance—he saw the dynamic clearly. Little by little, a small part of him was dying every day.

chapter fourteen

THE NEXT MORNING, HE was up a little earlier than usual. He had not been able to sleep much the past night, awakened every half hour or so by the recurring nightmare that had plagued him since his undergrad days at Howard. Nobody was chasing him, nor was he falling, or anything in the realm of *normal* nightmares like that. Instead he was tormented by a very realistic sensation of being in front of thousands of people and unable to say anything at all. An extremely terrifying nightmare for a motivational speaker to have.

His alarm was always set for eight o'clock, but this Friday he didn't need it. He showered, shaved, and sat down to his customary breakfast of cereal, hot chocolate, and his daily perusal of the *L.A. Times* sports section. He never started his day without checking the box scores, no matter what sport was currently in seasonal competition. And it was more than just a guy thing. It was practically a religion for him.

Forty-five minutes later he was in the Escalade and on his way to pick up Candace. He had made this same trip down Hollywood Freeway to Santa Monica Boulevard every day this week, but he had a canny little feeling that today would be different. Because today he had a bit of a surprise waiting for her after he finished his KKTL broadcast.

Much to his disappointment, her responses to his questions in this interview-stipulation game still remained guarded and somewhat clipped. She was answering his inquiries only to the point of giving just enough information, like he was a distant acquaintance who wasn't to be trusted with the intimate details. And that irked him because as each day passed, he was discovering that he wanted to get to know this young, Harlem Renaissance–esque sistah a lot better. Furthermore, she was attractive, intelligent, *and* opinionated—all added benefits he simply could not ignore. Her poised demeanor piqued his curiosity to the extreme because until now all the women's names in his black book were listed there because of what was between their legs and not their heads. But Candace Clark was . . . different. She was the first woman Jermaine had been around who actually made him consider turning in his "playa" card. And he could use such a lifestyle change because, according to his agent, there were far too many names in that book anyway. If the word ever leaked out to *StarWatch News* or some other bounty-hunting entertainment show about Jermaine's wild ways, the country might turn against its golden-voiced hero.

But his licentious habits were nothing more than mindless decoys—purely physical distractions that diverted his mind from the chaotic turmoil raging within his head. Without the fleshly pleasures he found in the arms of multiple women, he'd be . . . well, he'd be left with nothing but the dark, dreary reality of a dried-up fishbowl life.

He was at the hotel now and she was waiting, as usual, seated at the bar in the famed *Polo Lounge* restaurant. And equally typical, she was scribbling down something in her leather notebook portfolio.

Forever writin' something, ain't you?

"You ready, Candi?" He jangled his keys.

"My time's your time." She closed her notebook and swiveled off the bar stool. "Full schedule today, right?"

Jermaine grinned broadly. *If you only knew . . .*

• • •

ALL OF MYRA'S BUSINESS meetings for the current week had been conducted with incredible smoothness because with *Song of Solomon*'s rapidly growing stature as the hottest urban interest magazine in the country, there was no more red tape hindering her. She didn't have to jump through any more unnecessary hoops because of a lack of name recognition. No longer was she calling advertisers to practically beg them to patronize her magazine. Now, companies from all points on the economic spectrum were contacting her by the hour, literally falling over themselves for the chance to be listed in the next month's issue. "And for the right price you can have as big an ad as you want," came Myra's sharp business answer. The law of supply and demand was in effect, and for the first time, Myra

Washington was in demand. And that felt so, so good to her.

"Xavier, how's everything in your neck of the woods?" she asked as she drove north from the greater Atlanta area, heading to College Park to meet with her highly reputable, outsourced graphic designer. She was all set to okay the final cover proofs for July's issue.

"Busy as a blind beaver building a dam along the Mississippi. I think I've gotten like three hours' sleep all week."

"That's about two hours more than I've gotten. Sometimes I don't know how or where I'm getting the strength and energy to handle all these responsibilities."

"I know what you mean. But it's in moments like this when we realize God's grace is sufficient, don't we? We've got people all over the country praying for this venture, and I believe that's the main thing keeping us going. So, I'm hearing everything's ready now, that we're just waiting on Candace's interview."

"You're hearing correctly. I'm on my way to approve the layout right now. We've reserved four pages for the interview, with room for five photographs of Jermaine Hill, as well as the cover image."

"And the advertising?"

"It's been absolutely nothing but the favor of God working for us—listen to these figures. We've got twenty new three-year contracts, we re-signed all of our main sponsors, and we've got publicity spots running on two major television networks, as well as BET, TBN, and DayStar." Myra began to feel tingly all over, once again, just thinking about the incredible doors that had been opened to them. She knew that such opportunities had become possible purely through the favor and blessings given by the God whom she loved and served.

"Myra. Wow . . . I'm speechless . . . really, I mean what can I say to that except to God be the glory?"

"That's all that can or needs to be said, Xavier. Listen, I'll talk to you at the conference call meeting tonight, alright? Peace and blessings." She clicked off her cell and turned up the volume on her CD player, which at the moment was jamming Donald Lawrence and the Tri-City Singers gospel hit "The Best Is Yet to Come."

"How appropriate," Myra thought to herself. Because the best thing she could have imagined had indeed happened to her, and now it was time to reap the fruits of years and years of labor. And though she didn't have a voice that boasted of any singing prowess, she nevertheless joined in with the Tri-City Singers as the song went into its funky, urban vamp.

• • •

"HOW'D YOU LIKE THE show today?" Jermaine asked Candace as he approached her in the studio's green room. The live taping had gone off air about thirty minutes earlier.

She shrugged. "It could have been better."

"Could've been better—are you kiddin' me? I was flowin' like Run DMC out there. I tackled the subject of racism without rocking the politically correct boat of my diverse national audience. In my opinion, that's pretty good."

"Sometimes I wonder what *isn't* good in that much-inflated opinion of yours. Especially when it's taking cues from your ego." Then with much effort, she managed to smile appreciatively. "But alright, I admit—you walked through a virtual minefield today without blowing anything up. Bravo."

He took an exaggerated bow. "Thank you, thank you very much," he replied, lowering his voice to sound like Elvis Presley, not very successfully. At least his attempt elicited a smile from Candace.

"And for my next act of chivalry, I will endeavor to escort the esteemed Miss Candace Clark for an enjoyable afternoon of sightseeing and shopping along the Boardwalk."

"The Boardwalk? You mean Venice Beach? But . . . but what about your itinerary? It's extremely busy—I should know because I checked. You've got several corporate meetings today with—"

"I canceled everything," he cut in grandly. "Whether Mario liked that or not. He didn't, of course. Practically blew a couple of gaskets, but what do I care? Meetings can be rescheduled. But your time with me—my time with you—is only for one more week."

"That's true. But Jermaine, really. I don't want to come between you and your commitments. Face it, you're a busy man. Especially since—"

"I don't mean to cut you off twice in the same minute, but you're missing the point. I've already made up my mind to go to Venice today. Taking spontaneous breaks and getting away from all this madness is just as important to me as the meetings and shows.

It's a must. Shoot, if I don't get away sometimes . . . I don't know, I just may go crazy and kill myself." *Literally . . .*

Candace chuckled. "Well, we all need a break now and then. I certainly can understand that."

"So, what are we waiting for? C'mon." He led her out to the parking lot at the back of the studio, but instead of walking to his Escalade, he stopped beside a Honda motorcycle. Candace appeared surprised but she didn't say anything until he started removing the helmets lodged at the end of the leather seat.

"Jermaine, um . . . what are you doing?"

"About to take you to Venice Beach."

"No, I don't mean that. Why are you messing with this motorcycle? You're parked over there." She pointed in the direction of the luxury SUV.

"I'm also parked here." He affectionately patted the motorcycle. "This is my baby. A pure thrill machine. There's nothing like flying down the Santa Monica Freeway on one of these bikes, the wind blowing all around you. It's incredible. God, it's . . . it's true freedom, Candi. That's what it is. True freedom."

"Yeah, well, I don't ride motorcycles, thank you very much. So I'm sorry, but you're going to have to experience *true freedom* some other time."

Jermaine put down the helmet and turned toward her. "You're joking, right?"

Candace shook her head. "No."

"You've *never* ridden a motorcycle before?"

"No. These things are just too dangerous, and besides—"

"Now at least be sure and get the facts straight.

That's the first rule of journalism, right? Riding a motorcycle isn't nearly as dangerous as people always say it is. As far as accidents are concerned, the statistics are actually quite low."

"Yeah, but when an accident *does* happen, it doesn't take a genius to figure out the chances for survival are slim to none. There's no protection."

"I'm a good rider. And besides," he now put on a look of pure childlike innocence, "how are my fans supposed to truly know what I turn to when I'm looking for an escape? Isn't that what this interview was supposed to be about? A way for Jermaine Hill followers to connect with their hero?"

Candace rolled her eyes. "There you go, bringing out Mr. Ego again."

"I'm just saying—how are you going to accurately capture my true feelings unless you ride with me?" He grinned as he handed her a helmet. "I mean, it just makes good journalistic sense to me. Like those reporters who went over to the Middle East when we were at war. Bombs dropping all around them and everythin'. They could've wimped out, sure, but a true reporter does *whatever* it takes to get the story, right? So a single harmless motorcycle ride to Venice Beach shouldn't be a—"

"Alright, Jermaine." As she took the helmet, she gave him an icy look that said *proceed at your own risk.* "You've made your point already." Eyeing the helmet suspiciously, she added, "but if this thing messes up my hair, trust me, you don't even *want* to know the amount of pain I'll put you in."

• • •

THE WEATHER WAS simply beautiful for an afternoon at the beach, Candace slowly and somewhat reluctantly had to admit to herself. Living in Houston for all of her adult life, she was not at all used to temperatures in the mid-eighties without the irritating sidekick of stifling humidity. So the southern California breeze, bringing tantalizing mists of light saltwater showers to gently caress her face and skin, was quite the sensual experience for her.

And Jermaine, surprise of all surprises, turned out to be absolutely wonderful company. Gone were his egotistical opinions and commentaries that had tested her nerves all week. He was, to her newfound delight, thoughtful and sensitive as they shopped, fully taking in the quasi-Italian culture of Venice. As the evening progressed, they took a leisurely stroll along the beach. He answered all her questions openly and naturally without once resorting back to his little interview-stipulation game. And he hadn't even rubbed his chin on the hard questions she threw at him. It was a funny, almost strange thought to have, but as she walked beside Jermaine, she was plagued with a sense of guilt over the good time she was having. Guilt that she was out here, basking in the sunset off Venice Beach with Jermaine Hill, while her star-crazed best friend, Tasha, had literally dreamed of having moments such as this. Goodness, Tasha would kill to have a moment like this. But what did she have to feel guilty over? This was her job, right? She was strictly on assignment.

Assignment my behind . . . I'm starting to enjoy this . . .

"So, Jermaine, since we just cleared up the fact that the reason you're not married yet is because you haven't found someone to connect with on every level . . . can I assume that if you did find such a woman, you'd marry her?"

He appeared a bit surprised by the question. "Well, yeah. Why *wouldn't* I marry a woman like that?"

"Because some brothers are scared to commit, even if they have found someone who fulfills them on every level. Putting myself in the shoes and minds of your fans, I'm just curious to know what you would do."

"If I were to find such a woman?"

"Yes."

He rubbed his chin for the first time that day. "I'm not afraid of commitment. Not at all. And I think a love like that, between a man and a woman, is a beautiful thing, y'know?" Still rubbing his chin. "Yeah, I'd marry you . . . uh . . . I mean *her*." He began laughing nervously. "Yeah, I'd marry her."

You just say what I think you did? You did, didn't you? "So why are you so nervous talking about this? I mean, the great Jermaine Hill, the golden-voiced speaker who excites and inspires the country about life and all—I didn't think I'd ever get to see you nervous."

"I'm not nervous," he quickly retorted. Defensive, now.

"Oh, really?"

He cleared his throat and stuck his hands in his pockets. "Really." A second later he brought his right hand out and with it, skipped a penny along the shallow incoming waves of the Pacific Ocean. They walked along silently for another quarter mile or so. Candace had forgotten that she was still technically on an interview, and silently she relished her success in making Jermaine nervous. It was a small, but nonetheless significant victory for her. For she had finally broken through that macho wall of his to witness his genuine emotion. Arguably, it was the first honest emotion he had displayed so far this week.

"And what about you, Candace?"

Huh? "What . . . what about me?"

"You and your idea of Mr. Right. Prince Charming and all that. If you met a guy who connected with you on every level, and he proposed to you, you'd say yes?"

She didn't respond to the question right away. Such a question needed the proper amount of consideration before answering. "That's a highlight of a woman's life, you know? Being proposed to by the man she loves. And though some sistahs act like they're so independent and don't need a man, the truth of the matter is we all dream of that moment."

"I'll take that to mean you'd say yes."

"If he was Mr. Right, of course."

"What would make him Mr. Right?"

Aren't we curious all of a sudden . . . "Oh, I don't know."

"Don't get all coy on me—I've told you my idea of the perfect woman."

Candace laughed out loud. "Oh yeah right—and how sincere was that? Let me see if I can remember what this dream girl was like. The eyes of Vanessa

Williams, the figure of Janet Jackson, the legs of Tina Turner, and the brains of Condoleezza Rice. Puhleeze! A woman like that only exists in your dreams, Jermaine."

"Don't knock a brotha's dreams. For all we know, she could be out there somewhere."

"Yeah, well when you meet her, give me a call and let's all have lunch."

"Fabulous. We'll have a threesome."

She playfully punched him on the shoulder. "Watch it, my brotha."

Now it was his turn to laugh. "Alright, alright. Look, I promise to give you a more realistic description of my perfect woman if you describe to me your Mr. Right."

"You're serious?"

He nodded.

"Okay." She took her time and pretended to be deep in thought. Her act was all just a pretense though, because after her last nightmare of a boyfriend experience, she knew exactly what she now sought in a man.

"My Mr. Right would have to be willing to open up and be sensitive—to be unafraid to show his emotions."

Jermaine immediately made a face. "You mean, he'd have to cry and eat bon-bons while you forced him to watch Lifetime made-for-TV movies with you."

"No, I'm not saying that. Just that he'd be willing and unafraid to show emotions of all types in any given circumstance. Let's see, he'd also have to be educated and well read. And committed to exercising and eating right. He would have to believe in God and be able to grow spiritually with me. Oh, and of course, he would have to do the one thing *every* woman requires of her dream man."

Jermaine didn't even blink. "I know what that is."

Yeah, right . . . "You do? And what's that, oh great and all-knowing voice of inspiration?" She didn't mean to be sarcastic, but she knew she came off sounding that way.

"He would have to be able to make you laugh. Every real man knows that's the secret to winning a girl's heart." He looked over at her and smiled. "Am I right?"

By no means had she expected him to say that. "Um . . . well . . . yes. Yes, that's exactly right. How'd you know that?"

Almost instinctively, they both stopped walking. Facing her now, he stepped forward, almost into her personal space. "Let's just say that I have a way . . . of knowing things . . . like that." He leaned in much closer with just the right timing and kissed her tenderly and gently on the lips. It was the softest kiss Candace had ever felt. And it was incredibly sexy. Like luscious, creamy chocolate dusting her lips from a waterfall of sensuality somewhere above her. It was romantic and perfect. Just . . . *perfect*!

He pulled back after a few seconds. "Candi, I . . . I . . . Was I wrong to do that?" His voice, ever golden, now sounded a bit husky.

She couldn't think clearly. "N-no. Um . . . no. No, that was fine." *Do that again and I might go over the edge . . .*

Jermaine smiled and took her hand as they now

retraced their steps along the beach. On the horizon, the sun was setting majestically in the purplish, red-laced sky. To Candace the entire moment was like something right out of those old black-and-white movies on the AMC channel. Both of them were too caught up in the moment to say anything. So neither was aware of the man standing fifty-odd yards to their left, frantically snapping pictures of them like he was on some crude and secret photo shoot. In fact, they hadn't noticed that the man had been following them the entire afternoon and evening.

Ignorance is bliss, so goes the oft-quoted adage. But maybe the saying was all wrong. Maybe ignorance . . . was simply ignorance.

chapter fifteen

BY FAR, SUPER MARIO'S biggest client was Jermaine Hill, and accordingly the star speaker's never-ending affairs took just about every single minute of Mario's waking time to handle. Sponsor-hungry multimedia conglomerates daily bombarded his voice mail like persistent telemarketers. Corporations and civic organizations were forever after Jermaine to speak at their functions. His fame had progressed to the point that even select universities were now requesting that Jermaine give the keynote addresses for their commencements. More than anything, that last recognition had let Mario know his client was firmly entrenched at the top of the speakers' circuit. For who else had the crossover appeal that he did? Who else had the marketing versatility to speak to graduates from Ivy League colleges, rap to inner-city kids in America's ghettos, command and captivate a nationwide audience on public radio, and still be savvy enough to snag the largest book deal ever given to a motivational speaker? Mario Jordan was currently sitting on the hottest commodity on both Wall Street *and* Hollywood Boulevard, and he knew it. And not only that, before the last pages on the life of Jermaine Hill were written, Mario intended to make his client the wealthiest and most revered celebrity of the early twenty-first century. Because 15 percent of a financial portfolio of *that* gross magnitude wasn't half bad. Wasn't half bad at all.

The slow and steady vibration buzzing from the cell phone clipped to his belt awakened him from his daydreaming lapse about riches beyond his wildest dreams. He always kept his cell on vibrating mode; if he allowed the darn thing to ever ring, he'd never have any peace and quiet. For him, brokering ten to fifteen deals in an eight-hour business day was nothing at all.

"Mario here."

"Mr. Jordan, this is Perry Adams from UEAA. I was wondering if we can schedule your client for a power session with some investors after the general banquet this weekend."

"Perry, I've already informed you that Jermaine is leaving directly after he finishes speaking. We're on a very tight schedule this weekend; I don't see how delaying his departure would be possible."

"Mr. Jordan, I understand. However, United Entertainers is prepared to make this slight alteration to your plans financially worth your while."

Mario let a small laugh escape. At this stage in the negotiating game, it was simply and entirely about money. And he liked to think nobody talked a better bottom line than he did concerning dollars and cents. Still, Jermaine had been stubborn about his desire to leave right after the speech was over. Not that his client wanted to come back to L.A., though. Mario knew Jermaine secretly wanted to spend some time alone with that cute little writer. And not that Mario particularly cared—Candace Clark was not just another cheap floozy who might later blackmail his client. And Jermaine was a grown man—he could sleep with her if he wanted, as long as everything was kept tight, quiet, and most important, *discreet.*

"You say you can make this worth our while?"

"Yes, Mr. Jordan. *Significantly* worth any trouble you may encounter in reshuffling travel plans."

"Stay on the line, Perry. Let me get back to you in one minute." Mario picked up a cordless phone on his desk and dialed his client's number. He hoped Jermaine would pick up—Mario had instructed him to always answer when he called from the office.

"Jermaine Hill. Speak to me."

"J, I need to run something by you. Now I know you were very clear about wanting to go to that resort right after the banquet this weekend . . ."

"Yeah?"

". . . but Perry Adams basically just gave me a blank check to make an extra two hours very much worth our while. Two hours, J. What do you say? I know I can milk this guy's pockets for sixty grand, easy. Maybe even higher than that."

"Is everything always about money with you, Mario?"

"For Chrissake, J, I'm your *agent.* I'm supposed to look out for your financial interests and well-being. And I'm telling you this is a golden opportunity here. This is easier than stealing candy from a baby, for crying out loud! If I play my numbers right, I can put an extra seventy-five grand in the general account for just two more hours of your time. C'mon, J. Why am I begging you so hard on this? It's not even worth the breath to try and argue to the contrary."

"But staying two more hours puts Candi and me in Scottsdale much later than I planned to. We'd miss the whole evening."

"Will you listen to yourself, J? Candi and me. For the love of God, what is *that* about? Her stuff is that good to make you throw seventy-five grand away?" Mario could hardly believe this.

"Don't talk about her like that, Mario. You don't know her."

"I don't know her?" Mario was mad enough now to wring Jermaine's little golden-voiced neck. "She was a business acquisition, J! I hired her because she was the best writer out there to do this story. And now you go and get all Percy Sledge on her. I think spending all that time with her is messing with your brains, man."

"Yeah? Well I think all the money you're making off my voice is messing with *your* brains, Mario. For the last time, I'm leaving right after the banquet. End of discussion." Click.

Mario couldn't remember the last time he had been so furious. His client was definitely not himself, Candace Clark or no Candace Clark. Because nobody, but nobody, in their right mind would throw away a seventy-five-thousand-dollar opportunity over a woman. And it wasn't like he was asking Jermaine to sacrifice an entire evening. Just two freakin' hours. One hundred and twenty measly minutes. He looked up at his ceiling and cursed loudly and angrily for a full fifteen seconds.

"Hey, Perry? I'm back. Listen, we appreciate the generous offer from United Entertainers. But unfortunately, we're unable to make any changes to our plans."

"Mr. Jordan, I . . . I . . ." Mario didn't think Perry Adams was the kind of person who stuttered much in his business deals, but he guessed there was a first time for everything.

". . . I just don't understand," he finally managed to say.

"Join the club, Perry my friend." *You'd be amazed at all the card-carrying members* . . . "I'll see you tomorrow evening."

• • •

ON THE TELEVISION screen in front of her, Andy Griffith was doing his clever best to fix Barney up with a shy woman who made her living as a seamstress. Andy had even gone so far as to stage a minor robbery to make the incompetent Barney Fife look like a hero. *"Poor Barney,"* Bell thought to herself, smiling. The bumbling little deputy never could do anything right for himself.

The black-and-white images flickering on the small set in front of her transported her back in time to the 1960s. Life was so much simpler then. She certainly had fewer headaches and stress, that was for sure. In those days, she had nothing on her mind but going to church and cooking and cleaning for that nice little family who had treated her so well.

What were their names? Such a nice, loving family . . . oh my Lordy, has it been that long? Or . . . or is it just my mind . . .

Of course, Bell knew the answer to that depressing question. She also knew that she didn't have much time left, now. But there wasn't any sense of fear gripping her over such a realization; quite the contrary—she was in fact ready to go home to be with her blessed Savior. To be absent from the body was to be present with the Lord. So she was . . . well, she was *almost* ready. There was still something she longed to see realized.

"Save my son, Jesus . . ." she whispered. "Save my Jermaine." She wished it were that simple, like life had been forty years earlier. But this wasn't Mayberry. She had never lived in that sleepy little town, anyway.

• • •

"GIVE ME SOME more details, Candi! You gave Jermaine my picture and number like I asked, right?"

Candace adjusted the phone cradled between her neck and shoulder, stalling for time. She was feeling more than a little guilty because it had been only yesterday when she'd been walking, hand in hand, along Venice Beach with the man. Come to think of it, she'd been doing more than just walking.

"Um . . . no, not yet. But don't worry, I'll get around to it."

"You better get around to it! 'Cause I've got a real good feeling about this guy, you know? Jermaine Hill could be *the* one for me, I don't care what you have to say about it."

Oh, please . . . "That's great, Tasha. So how about you, hmm? How've you been?"

"The usual. Work, home, Blockbuster night, work, home—you know how it is."

"Didn't you get that promotion you were—"

"Hey, I didn't call long distance to talk about me. I want to hear some more juicy details about my man."

"Well, there's really nothing new to—"

"Oh, no you don't! Don't be holding out on me, sis. Have you ever known me to hold out on you in the ten years we've been friends?"

Have I ever known you to keep a secret longer than a minute? "No, Tasha. You've always been liberal with dishing out information."

"You see? Now why should you be any different with me?"

Candace sighed, placed her phone on speaker, and began giving her friend a recap of her past couple of days. Well, with one exception, of course.

I'll be keeping the Venice Beach details to myself, girlfriend . . .

chapter sixteen

THE LAST TIME CANDACE had the pleasure of visiting Phoenix, Arizona, it was for a chance to interview then–Phoenix Suns basketball star Kevin Johnson. Candace was still in high school, writing for the *Dallas Morning News*, and a feature article in the works about athletes and entertainers giving back to their respective communities had fallen to her. Fortunately, just a few weeks prior to that, she had been reading about the basketball player establishing the St. Hope Academy, a PS7 charter school, in his Sacramento, California, hometown. She was personally intrigued by the story because one of her cousins had grown up in the Oak Park section of Sacramento and was now volunteering at the school. Ever the resourceful go-getter, Candace had persuaded the newspaper to fly her to Phoenix to interview KJ after a game. Not only had KJ been a great interview (and Candace's first of many crushes), but she also had immensely enjoyed touring the capital of the Grand Canyon State. She felt wondrously alive in the arid climate and amid desert wildlife, visually taking in the hilly landscapes and learning the Spanish culture. And though it wasn't exactly in the designated travel budget, she had driven north up to Grand Canyon National Park afterward where she was awed at that cavernous, breathtaking design of nature. Some of the best poetry she had ever written had been penned while beholding the mammoth rock formations of one of the great wonders of the world.

"You had a crush on Kevin Johnson?" Jermaine asked, his eyebrows raised, as they dined in the Terrace Café of the Hyatt Regency in downtown Phoenix. It was approaching two in the afternoon, and they were just finishing up a delicious brunch.

"Yes. So? What's wrong with that? KJ was handsome, courteous, and basically just a very nice guy all around. And I'm sure you've even had crushes on famous . . . wait a minute, what am I talking about? You *are* famous. So what about when you were in school? Didn't you have any adolescent crushes?"

"If you put it that way, yeah I guess. Growing up, I always had a thing for . . ." He stopped in midsentence, shaking his head. Candace could tell he was mentally calculating how much he wanted to tell.

"For who?" she pressed. Her journalistic instincts were taking over, and she just had to know—this would definitely be vital information for her story. That is, if he trusted her enough to be that revealing.

He sheepishly grinned as he muttered, "Claire Huxtable."

"Claire Huxtable? Claire—oh, you mean the actress from *The Cosby Show*? Jermaine, she played the *mother*, for goodness sake!" She couldn't help but laugh.

"That's right—laugh it up, Candi. I mean, what in

the world would be so attractive about an intelligent black woman who's a lawyer, funny, witty, and a great mother to boot. Plus, Phylicia Rashad was a fine woman to begin with."

"Hmmph . . . well, if you put it that way . . ."

"Yeah, I most certainly put it that way, Miss KJ." It was his turn now to laugh. At the sound of his laughter, she flashed him a warning look. She wasn't about to be teased for something as silly as a teenage infatuation.

"So you follow basketball, then? Or you just have a thing for good-looking athletes?"

Hmm . . . both, really . . . She kept that thought to herself. "I don't mind a good game of hoops now and then."

"Really? That's surprising. I wouldn't have pictured you as the type."

"The type, huh? Well I wouldn't have pictured *you* as the type that goes for older women." She had exactly two seconds to duck before Jermaine purposely tossed a wadded-up paper napkin at her. And he had even less time before she sent the thing, missile-like, back in his direction.

• • •

"SPIKE, YOU ARE the man!" Chantal punched the air with her fist as she reviewed the eight-by-ten-sized photographs of Candace Clark and Jermaine Hill openly cavorting along the sands of Venice Beach. Even if Spike didn't get any more pictures of them at that Arizona resort this weekend, what Chantal was now looking at was more than enough damaging material to corroborate her scandalous story.

"Oh, this is good . . . this is good . . . this is *so* good!" She was almost delirious as the near-paralyzing emotions of revenge, euphoria, and ecstasy oozed from every pore in her body. Never in her life had she felt so satisfied . . . so fulfilled . . . so complete. She took her investigative reporting job very seriously and with the story she was about to circulate, pretty soon the whole country was going to take *her* very seriously as well. She'd be right up there in name recognition with Barbara Walters, with Diane Sawyer, and with the ultra-rich Katie Couric. But the new girl on the block wouldn't have near the respectable image those news veterans possessed. No, to the contrary, *she* would be the most feared woman in journalism! Chantal Dixon—the reporter who knew more dirt about the stars than anyone else.

Take that, Mario Jordan!

"Look out everybody, I'm about to destroy the image of your little golden-voiced wonder," she crowed as she held up one of the photographs. The print clearly showed Jermaine and Candace kissing and embracing much like two Shakespearean star-crossed lovers. The image was romantic if one didn't know the couple's identities.

But those two people were currently at the center of Chantal's witch hunt, and she was primed and ready to expose the serious conflict-of-interest problem with Candace interviewing Jermaine. Not only that, but she also had a serious vendetta to expose Jermaine's lesser-known lothario tendencies. She had been secretly contacting some girls in Hollywood who, for the right price, would spill their stories about how Jermaine Hill had loved them and left them. How the country's voice of inspiration secretly had more one-night stands than a bad comedian trying to get a laugh on *Def Comedy*. This man was going down, that much she knew. Chantal Dixon was willing to bank her entire career just to ensure it.

• • •

UNITED ENTERTAINERS Association of America sought to provide representation and benefits for thousands of "starving artists," so to speak—such people being the many B- and C-grade actors, musicians, and singers who couldn't afford the same representation that the top artists in their fields enjoyed. Jermaine had first gotten involved with UEAA when he, too, was a struggling artist during his last few semesters at Howard. On many cold nights and long winter weekends, he had paid his dues riding the buses up and down the East Coast to speak at various engagements. On many of those nights, he'd been the most gracious recipient of some sound legal advice and marketing assistance from the association. Advice that had proven to be quite significant early on in his career. And of course, now that he had "arrived" as the top inspirational speaker in the country, the red welcome carpet was always laid out for him to address the annual UEAA banquet.

The main exhibit hall of the Phoenix Civic Plaza Convention Center was packed to capacity, all 220,000 square feet of newly constructed available space. And every listener was sitting literally on the edge of his or her seat, absorbing everything their hero and fellow member was dishing out. They had reason to—Jermaine was in rare form this afternoon.

"Every one of you who is dreaming of making it big, let me tell you this—you have *got* to hold on to that dream. Even if nobody else believes in you. And especially if nobody supports you or thinks you're capable of making it to the big time. Because, ask yourself this question—what *is* the big time, exactly? Is it to have your film shatter the opening box-office records? Is it to have your music album go platinum? Your book to be at the top of all the best-seller lists? Would that make you big time, then?"

He took a deep breath as he scanned the thousands of people jam-packed in the cavernous meeting hall. By their facial expressions, he could tell that in their minds those types of accolades would have indeed announced their arrival on the coveted A-list. But how little they knew. They could have all of that, could taste success beyond their wildest dreams, and still have . . . absolutely nothing.

I should know, 'cause here I am, world. The biggest hypocrite in the history of motivational speaking . . .

"Let me tell you something, UEAA. Let me tell you when you've really arrived and reached the big time. It's when you can look in the mirror at the end of the day and smile because you like what's lookin' back at you. It's when you don't care what anyone says about your film, song, or book because you know you gave that project one hundred and ten percent. You've reached the big time when you're lovin' what you do.

And doin' what you love." He paused to flash his winning smile. "But don't get me wrong—it don't hurt to get paid doing it, either!"

The audience applauded with near-fanatical fervor, taking in his words like they were being passed down as the Holy Grail. They were so eager and ready to be in his shoes, to be drunk with the success and prestige that he apparently was basking in. But while Jermaine was flashing his smile and quoting his wonderful little phrases, inside he was growing sick of the horrific irony. If these people wanted his life, then they didn't know what they were asking for. Because there was no way they could fathom the kind of hell he was experiencing, even though he was supposedly living out his childhood dream.

He felt hopelessly alone in the midst of thousands of adoring supporters. He'd never really felt true love except from his old Aunt Bell, Ronny, and Eric. His two homeboys were gone. And Aunt Bell, God rest her poor soul, might as well have been gone—Alzheimer's disease had so ravaged her mind a few years ago that Jermaine found it extremely difficult to visit her. So his dilemma was not just a perceived problem; he in fact *was* alone. Popular, successful, adored, wealthy . . . but nevertheless, alone.

He had one bright thought shining through his fog of despair, though. Jermaine had sensed that Candace, like a budding rose, was gradually opening up her heart to him. Their romantic walk along Venice Beach yesterday had done much to persuade him that she might be more than just a writer interviewing him. Oh yes, she could very well be much, much more than that.

chapter seventeen

JERMAINE, I'VE GOT to tell you—you have got one heck of an effect on your audiences. It's kind of electrifying." Candace looked over at him in the limousine's backseat and wagged a finger at him. "And I don't easily dish out praise, but . . ."

He stuck out his chest. "But I'm the man, huh?"

Easy, easy on the testosterone, there . . . She laughed. "Um, something like that." She took a sip of ginger ale from the glass tumbler on the tray in front of her. From that evening they were first introduced, Jermaine had honored her wishes to not have alcoholic beverages in her company. It could seem like a small matter to some, but Candace had greatly respected him for faithfully adhering to that stipulation.

"So where are we headed?" she asked. "I noticed the last-minute changes to the itinerary—you've got the next two days somewhat blocked off. Why the change?"

Jermaine leaned back in his seat. "I just needed some time off. The body can wear down, y'know? I haven't had a chance to really relax all week, and there's this great little resort up in Scottsdale that's perfect for a little R&R."

"Oh. Oh, well . . . that sounds nice, I guess."

"You don't mind, do you? I mean, I kind of booked this resort for the both of us. It's been a busy week for you as well."

"Yes, it's definitely been busy. But I'm on assignment here. I knew these two weeks were going to be hectic when I agreed to do this."

"Is that all I am?" He glanced over at her, the expression on his face a mixture of surprise and mischief. "An *assignment*?"

Candace took another sip of ginger ale, giving her a few extra seconds to stall. Without a doubt, she would have to answer this question carefully. "No, Jermaine, of course not. I mean, at first . . . I, well . . . I didn't know you. You were just another public figure to me, just another celebrity interview. And you guys . . . I mean, uh, *some* celebrities can be real pricks, you know? Completely insensitive and stuck on thinking the world revolves around them. Now, I try to give everyone the benefit of the doubt, but you just never know sometimes."

Jermaine chuckled and shook his head.

"What? What's so funny?"

"Oh, nothing. You just didn't answer the question, is all. Danced all around it, but didn't answer it."

"Well, I didn't mean to . . ."

"Then don't." He leaned forward and a little closer to her. "So tell me, Candi. Am I . . . just another assignment . . . to you?"

Candace felt her heart beating a little faster. Closer

to him now than she'd been all night, she was overtaken by his scent—the tantalizing combination of his designer cologne, the pomade he rubbed on his close-cropped hair, the rich smell of his imported, Italian suit—it was all sensually overwhelming. And exciting.

"No, Jermaine . . ." Her voice was barely audible now, and she could feel the blood pounding in her head. "No, of course you're not just an assignment to me."

With his finger, he tilted her chin up so that she was looking directly into his eyes. Candace's senses were so on fire that she imagined she would explode any second now. Every sound, every smell, every taste . . . was incredibly and magnificently heightened.

"That night on the beach changed all that, didn't it?" he asked. "You and me, walking together hand in hand. Something happened, right? I *know* I wasn't the only one who felt something."

Candace opened her mouth to say something, but the words stuck in her throat. As Jermaine gazed earnestly into her eyes, with his finger he slowly started to stroke the soft spot just under the bottom of her chin. The effect was mesmerizing, and Candace wished she could bottle up that moment and preserve it for the rest of her life. Every woman, she thought to herself, ought to have a "princess" moment like this at least once in her lifetime.

"You felt it, didn't you, Candi?" Still stroking her chin.

She swallowed and after a minute or so, she finally felt strong enough to respond. "Y-yes. Yes, Jermaine, I did feel something."

• • •

THE LAVISH SUITE at the Phoenician Resort was already prepared for Candace and Jermaine, and as they walked through the double doors she immediately took note of the partially dimmed lights and the soft, mellow jazz playing somewhere in the room.

"I know this song . . . Boney James playing 'Sweet Thing' . . ."

Jermaine nodded as he set his small bag down on a plush sofa chair. "Yeah. A little bird told me you liked jammin' to his music. The cat's alright on the sax, I guess. But when we get back to L.A., I'm gonna have to hip you to some Duke Ellington. Take you back to the roots of jazz."

Playfully, she rolled her eyes. "Whatever, Jermaine." Walking to the window, she proceeded to look out over the hilly, desert landscape. Her mind went back in time to her vacation of sorts, years ago when she did that interview here for the *Dallas Morning News*. She had such fond memories of this city, partially because of Kevin Johnson, partially because of . . . because of . . .

Go ahead and admit it, girl. You're starting to like Jermaine, aren't you?

But what about her story? And for God's sake, what about Tasha? Now wouldn't *that* just go over well—to go back to Houston only to have her best friend find out that she and Jermaine were now a hot item. Tasha would definitely throw a fit the size of Texas. Still, yesterday at the beach . . . and then just a few minutes ago in the limousine, Candace had discovered that she had

. . . well, she had *feelings* for this guy. Feelings that probably weren't going away any time soon.

"Arizona is really beautiful, isn't it?" Jermaine asked as he slowly walked up behind Candace. "If you'd like, we can go up to the Grand Canyon later. Take one of those helicopter tours or something."

"Yes. Yes, that'd be nice." She turned around and found herself, once again, extremely close to Jermaine.

Oh, God . . . oh God . . . oh . . .

Her heart started furiously beating faster. And her now-shallow breaths began to come in short little spurts.

Seeming to sense her nervousness, Jermaine once again reached out and began to stroke the spot just under her chin. "Candi, just . . . just relax, okay?" His golden voice was smooth and reassuring. "I'm not going to do anything you don't want me to."

"Aren't you the perfect gentleman."

He slowly shook his head. "No, I'm not perfect. Far from it, in fact. But all I know is that right here, right now . . . I just want to be with you." He slowly dropped his hand from her chin, and with his other arm, he now circled her waist.

"Candi, you are such a beautiful woman. And y'know something else? You're also one of the most intelligent and well-spoken sistahs I've ever met."

"I'll take that as sort of a compliment because I've . . . uh, heard that you've met *a lot* of women, Jermaine."

He looked disappointed. "Don't believe everything you hear. I mean sure, because of my hectic schedule I meet a few ladies here and there, but *nobody* has had quite the effect that you've had on me."

"What kind of effect is that?"

"Hmm . . . now let me see. Well first off, you have a way of looking past the front I normally put up for people. It's like you can really see into me. And while that scared me at first, now I kind of like it. Plus, you're successful, independent, driven, talented . . . shall I go on?"

"Yes . . ." she breathed, mercifully relieving some of her built-up inner tension. But her heart was still beating at a rapid rate. Jermaine's wonderful, manly scent and physique were creating blissful havoc in her mind. "Please do go on."

He pulled her even closer to his broad chest, and now she could feel the fluttering of *his* heart, which was beating just as fast as hers.

"And you are definitely, absolutely the finest sistah writing books that I've ever met." He tilted his face to hers, now certainly about to kiss her.

"I . . . I really don't write books . . . I write features . . ." she began saying.

"Whatever." His ensuing kiss started off with just the right amount of tenderness, escalating with each fleeting second into such a passionate embrace that Candace thought her poor little heart was going to pass out.

After a while, Jermaine slowly pulled back, only to then bend down and pick her up. With her secured daintily in his arms, he headed for the bedroom.

"Jermaine . . . Jermaine, wait . . ." she softly whispered. Oh, but this felt so right and so good! And she *knew* that if she let this continue, it would be a wonderful night that she'd never forget. But . . . was she ready for this? And what about Tasha?

Oh, to heck with that crazy girl . . .

So if not Tasha, then what about her article? Whether she liked it or not, she was first and foremost a professional who had always adhered to the unwritten literary code of ethics. Sleeping with Jermaine tonight might indeed feel good but it would compromise *everything* she had learned from Dr. West back at Rice. And it would call into question everything she believed in as a writer on a quest to win a Pulitzer someday. But she had already sacrificed so much to get to this point. What was one harmless little night of sensual indulgence going to hurt?

By this point, Jermaine had undone nearly all the buttons on the back of her knit blouse and was slowly caressing her bare shoulders with his hands and mouth, working his way down her arms.

"Jermaine, wait . . ."

He groaned and with a near-Herculean effort, pulled away from her shoulders. "Candi, what's wrong? Tell me what I'm doing wrong."

"Oh, Jermaine, you're doing nothing wrong. It's . . . it's me . . . I'm not ready for th— I mean, I just can't do this."

He groaned again.

"It's . . . it's just not right," she continued. "Not only is there a serious conflict of interest going on here, but . . . well, I'm still kind of an old-fashioned girl."

With a show of great reluctance, he pulled farther away from her, to where he was now lying next to her on the bed. "But don't you *feel* this? I mean, doesn't this whole evening, this whole weekend, just feel *right* for you and me?"

"I . . . I don't know." *Girl, you are crazy! You got a fine man who's ready to worship your body all night long and you tell him you don't know?* "Jermaine, listen, you're a really great guy, but . . ."

He immediately held up his hands. "Un-unhh. Not the *'you're a great guy, but'* run-around."

"Jermaine, I didn't mean it like that. Really. But right now, with this interview and everything, I just don't think this will work."

"Aren't you about through with the interview already? I mean, you've been following me around all week—I'm sure you've got plenty of material to work with by now." He leaned forward to kiss her once more, but she pulled away. More firmly this time. It was one of the hardest things she had done, because her body was physically screaming for his touch.

"Jermaine, no. Please . . . please . . ." After an awkward few seconds, she asked, "um . . . is there another room I can go to? I saw that you only had one room booked, and . . ."

"Well that was because—"

"I know, I know. I'm sorry, Jermaine." She wrapped her arms around herself, suddenly feeling a chill. Undoubtedly because her blouse was still open at the back.

"You don't have to go anywhere, Candi. You can stay in this room. I'll leave." He leaned in for a final kiss, but stopped halfway, letting out a dejected sigh as he did so. Then he got up from the bed and left the room.

All alone now, Candace thought it so strange that even though he was the one who had walked out the door, for some inexplicable reason, *she* felt like she was the one leaving something behind.

chapter eighteen

JERMAINE PERSONALLY TOOK the limo and drove himself in the direction of the Grand Canyon, with the window down to let the onrushing dry wind fly in his face. A dust storm could have blown in his eyes for all he cared. It was a good thing there was practically no traffic at this late hour because he wasn't particularly alert; just about all he was presently conscious of were the yellow dividing lines on the highway. His rag-tag thoughts were a veritable wasteland of confusion.

It wasn't the fact that he had been rejected by a woman, although *that* hadn't happened for quite some time now. Because for him, getting a girl to spend the night with him was like getting a late-night appetizer from a drive-thru window, crude as that analogy was. No, it was the rejection by Candace Clark that had driven the stake right through his heart. Why did he have to be rejected by *her*? The one person with whom he had finally felt comfortable enough to open up and be semitransparent. The one woman for whom he had considered turning in his "playa" card. The one lady who had earned and won his respect and admiration.

Emotions of pain, bitterness, and loneliness that had dominated his life over the past ten years now played in his mind like a horrible, grainy, silent black-and-white movie. And the images he saw were far from comforting: being virtually abandoned by his good-for-nothing parents; Ronny's and Eric's tragic deaths; Aunt Bell's Alzheimer's disease and now almost-imminent death. It seemed the only people in his godforsaken world who had ever cared about him were either dead, dying, or had forgotten his existence altogether.

You're back in the freakin' fishbowl again, with nowhere to swim . . .

As he bumbled along the dusty Arizona highway, he was more consumed with feelings of self-pity and depression now than he'd ever been. More than likely, *nobody* would ever come to know the true Jermaine Hill; this thought crept into his fragile mind with the subtleness of the serpent of old. Who would ever know that he longed for quiet nights of slow jazz and strawberry lemonades? Or that he was an avid film buff who could recite, verbatim, the Academy Award winners for Best Film over the past thirty years? Who would know the quiet, relaxed side of him that actually cared very little for the limelight and fame? Or that he would *gladly* trade in his seemingly wonderful life for the simple pleasures of a good friend, a woman he could love and grow old with, and a son for whom he could be the Daddy he himself never had?

And maybe that's it . . . maybe nobody's gonna know . . .

He was now back to entertaining the very real and very haunting contemplation of suicide that had darkened his thoughts for the better part of a year. Before then, he had always thought it plain crazy to try and take one's own life. Because why in the world would somebody want to do that?

But he now knew why. He was a prime candidate, ripe with all the telltale symptoms. He had no friends—just agents, lawyers, and a horde of bloodthirsty acquaintances who were forever vying to have a little more of his "juice." Millions of people loved and practically worshiped him for being somebody he honestly was *not.* Nobody knew him for the person he in fact really was. And at this rate, finding such a person was just about impossible because even he couldn't remember who that guy was. He had acted the golden-voiced boy routine so much and so long that he hadn't realized just how convincing he had become in doing so.

Yeah, well . . . the act is over, kid . . .

He drove on, resolutely and despairingly committed to once and for all ending this stupid little charade called life.

chapter nineteen

THE FAX CAME TO Myra's attention at just past three in the morning. In a normal week, she would have been blissfully tucked away in her Victorian-style bed, somewhere drifting through the contented clouds of dreamland. But this had been far from a typical week, and so at this early hour she was still e-mailing various news contacts, briefing them on *Song of Solomon*'s added distribution channels. She had just commenced typing the last sentence to an executive in New York when her fax machine started humming, signaling an incoming message. She retrieved the first page and after reading the content knew immediately that her busy week was about to become much busier. And much worse as well.

"Oh, my God . . ." For a second, she was overcome with lightheadedness and thought she might pass out. After a while the dizziness was gone, although the nightmare of what she had just read was merely beginning.

To: Myra Washington, Editor in chief
Re: Notification of photograph release to all interested parties

StarWatch News, Inc. has obtained eight pictures of Mr. Jermaine Hill and Miss Candace Clark, revealing these two individuals in a compromising situation and bringing into question the credibility of their upcoming interview. SWN's own award-winning reporter, Chantal Dixon, has been gathering evidence for an exclusive story that will . . .

The memo went on in greater detail, but Myra's eyes immediately darted to the next page as it was coming out of the facsimile machine. It was unmistakably a picture of Jermaine and Candace in the throes of an extremely passionate embrace along a beach somewhere.

Oh, my God . . .

The pictures were by no means obscene, risqué, or anything of an X-rated sort. But because of *who* they were, and the horrible timing of such a release, Myra knew the pictures had the potential to be extremely damaging. So damaging, in fact, that they could very well upstage the release of *Song of Solomon*'s much-anticipated feature. And everything that she had worked so hard for, all that she had hoped and dreamed for this magazine would be wasted just like *that*. She grabbed her phone and punched in Xavier's number.

"Xavier, you there?"

"Mm . . hmmm," came his sleepy reply as she heard him loudly yawn with the same breath. "Barely. And wouldn't you know it—this is my first sleep in about two weeks and naturally, it gets interrupted."

"Sorry about that, but it can't be helped. You're going to be wide awake after you hear this, anyway. Chantal Dixon and *StarWatch News* are about to publish some pictures and a story about Jermaine and Candace . . . about them being *lovers.*"

"W-what?"

"I had the same reaction. But I'm thinking it might be true. I'm looking at a fax of one picture of the two of them together right now."

"Oh, man. Oh . . . this isn't good."

"Xavier, this is catastrophic!" Her voice, normally steady and sure, now bordered on a desperate wail. "Whether these allegations are true or not, the gossip mill is going to hit us regardless, before our feature is even printed!" Myra was so upset that she could cry.

"Wait a minute, Myra. We need to stay calm and think this through. No, actually, we need to pray. We're definitely going to need God's direction and guidance about how to handle this issue."

She knew Xavier was right about the praying (as he most always was), but at the moment her emotions were taking over. "I'm . . . I'm just too upset to pray. You're going to have to do it for the both of us. The rumors about Chantal doing anything to scoop a story are unfortunately true." *The nerve of that meddling Chantal Dixon!*

"Alright," Xavier calmly replied. "Father, in the name of Jesus . . ." He proceeded to fervently begin calling on help from on high, but Myra was near oblivious to the intercession of her friend and colleague.

Though she was a woman normally not given to letting her emotions rule, somehow the floodgates were open all the way with this current bombshell. How dare her golden opportunity be tarnished by a scum-dwelling, bottom-feeding, celebrity leech of a reporter with a twisted vendetta! And though she felt it was mostly Chantal Dixon's fault, she had to admit that those pictures had definitely *not* been staged. Meaning that Candace Clark was a little at fault as well for compromising her journalistic ethics and causing a cloud of doubt to now hang over the whole interview. Such a grave mistake might have been tolerated in a greenhorn or novice, but this girl was one of the most promising young writers in the country. How in the world could Candace have allowed something like this to happen?

As Xavier continued praying, Myra's mind frantically fast-forwarded into damage-control mode. How could she salvage this story? She was already 25 percent over the budget on preproduction, and her sole rationale had been the edition's selling hot off the press, as the old saying went. But now, if the media began saying that this story was biased or tainted in any way, not only would such rumors affect sales, but they also would do great damage to the moral image and standard she sought to uphold with *Song of Solomon*.

"So Lord, we know that Your plans will be established throughout these upcoming days, and we place our complete and unwavering faith in You to see us through . . ."

Perhaps Xavier's faith was complete and unwavering at the moment, but Myra's was far from it. Her faith was currently rockier than an off-the-Richter scale southern California earthquake.

chapter twenty

THE STORY FIRST BROKE on StarWatch's Sunday morning cable television show with a two-minute lead-in featuring Chantal Dixon openly reveling in the Woodward and Bernstein–like fervor of scooping such a national-interest story. The pictures of Jermaine and Candace's romantic romp along Venice Beach were soon copied and forwarded to the other morning news shows and pretty soon a definite media slant began to emerge. The inference was that Candace Clark had been singled out for the interview because she and Jermaine had been secret lovers for years. Further, the media suggested that not only had Mario Jordan known about this clandestine relationship, but so had *Song of Solomon* magazine—which could explain how a small and relatively obscure magazine had landed the biggest feature of the year. The media pundits that flooded the morning talk show circuits debated: if the media's slants were true, then both the magazine and Candace could ensure that the story cast only a positive and glowing light on Jermaine.

KKTL Radio opted to have no comments about the

whole affair except to state that they would grant their star host the courtesy and freedom to issue his own statement.

Mario Jordan could not be reached at either his home or office, but sent word to the television networks that his client was nothing more than a libel victim of a publicity-crazed reporter. When all the facts had been gathered and disseminated, he argued, they would show that his client's involvement with Candace Clark was purely a business relationship, and that Jermaine had conducted his affairs with the utmost integrity.

The statement issued by *Song of Solomon* magazine was written along the same lines as Mario Jordan's, but whether the country believed these various spin-control efforts remained to be seen.

Perhaps the *one* person entirely oblivious to the swirling media controversy was the man directly in the center of it. He had not seen the morning shows or read any of the Sunday newspapers. After traveling up to the Canyon, Jermaine had then somehow found his way back to I-10 and taken it due west. Six hours later, just before ten o'clock, he found himself in the familiar outskirts of Los Angeles. All along the early-morning drive, he had been mulling over a crude plan that had grown like an oversize weed in his mind for the past year. And though he had wondered before if he had the guts to carry out such a fanatical scheme, the previous night's rejection from Candace proved to be the last bit of ammunition he needed to put it in place.

It was a crazy and daring idea. He would jump off a point on Mount Lee, the highest peak in L.A., famous for the Hollywood sign perched on its hills, and mercifully plummet to his passageway out of his godforsaken fishbowl. He would have liked to jump off one of the fifty-foot letters themselves, but sophisticated security had been added to arguably the most famous sign in the world after a disappointed young star-in-waiting named Peg Entwhistle had jumped to her death in 1932 from the letter "H." Though that tragedy had taken place many years before, Hollywood was determined never to have a repeat occurrence. Hiking to the sign now was strictly prohibited and motion detectors had been placed all over the usual pathways; any alarms were now sure to bring quick responses from LAPD helicopters. But Jermaine chose not to make a huge deal out of a small issue. There were a number of points on Mount Lee high enough, and most important, *symbolic* enough, to convey the message he wished to send. Which was—that for all the glitz and glamour the Hollywood lifestyle offered, in the end the whole thing only proved to be a bittersweet façade. It was like an entertaining movie perhaps that, despite all its thrills and wonders, inevitably ended in sobering tragedy. It was exactly as Marilyn Monroe had said: "Hollywood is a place where they'll pay you $50,000 for a kiss and 50 cents for your soul."

Turning off Beachwood Drive, he parked the limousine as inconspicuously as possible and headed on foot to the path that would take him around the south bend of the rugged mountain. His mind was numb as he plodded along the trail, refusing to let any second guesses pollute his stubborn and dead-set will. He was going to do this because he was tired of living life in a fishbowl. Tired of the constant demands to his time, the invasion of privacy whenever he was out among the public, of giving daily encouragement and motivation to the whole nation but receiving absolutely *nothing* in return. Tired of having no one to reveal his heart to, nobody to whom he could sincerely confide his doubts and fears. Tired of having no one to love . . . and no one to love him. So what if jumping to his death would be perceived as cowardly to most people? They weren't in his shoes and they certainly did not have his problems. Not that Jermaine particularly cared about the opinions of others, anyway. All he knew was that he was boarding a one-way train out of this miserable little life.

• • •

IF EVER THERE WERE medals given out acknowledging dedication and persistence in the world of private investigating, then in Spike's mind, he would be a prime candidate for top honors. From his vantage point in the adjacent suite to Jermaine and Candace's room at the Phoenician, he had observed Jermaine's surprising departure a little after midnight. Stranger still was the fact that the man had taken the keys to the limo and driven himself over three hundred miles to Los Angeles, leaving Candace and his own chauffeur both behind. In Spike's line of work he had come across many puzzling people and actions, but this act made absolutely no sense at all.

At any rate, proving to be quite the persisent little sleuth, Spike had followed Jermaine along the bizarre drive on I-10, managing to stay far enough behind to avoid detection. Behind Jermaine, he arrived in L.A. and headed toward Hollywood Hills. Spike put a call through to Chantal once he saw the star speaker park the limo and proceed traveling on foot.

"Chantal. Baby, you ain't gonna believe this. Our lover boy left Candace behind in Phoenix, drove to L.A., and is now walking north on Beachwood. Looks like he's headed toward the hills. This boy is definitely a class-A weirdo."

"What?" Chantal gulped down the last of her coffee—only her second cup for that morning—and turned away from her computer monitor. Still riding the euphoric wave of being the one to break the scandalous story currently dominating the AP wire, she was not sure she had heard her source correctly. "Run that by me again, Spike?"

"Jermaine Hill is, as I speak, making his way up Mount Lee *on foot*. He rolled out of Phoenix just after midnight last night and drove himself here for some reason. Now, why he's doing this—I ain't got a clue at all."

"Hmm. This could be good . . . this could be good," Chantal purred as her ever-publicity-seeking mind once again kicked in and shifted into overdrive. "Maybe we can work his odd behavior to our advantage, because the press has been calling every half hour, asking us if we know anything about Jermaine's whereabouts." She punched the air with her fist. "Yes, yes . . . yes! We can get the scoop again! We can take those paparazzi fools right to the source himself! You say he's walking on Mount Lee right *now*, Spike?"

"Yeah. I'm right behind him."

"Good, good . . ." She turned back to her computer and began accessing her files for contacts of the people in the press corps most likely to follow up on this tip. "Keep tailing him, Spike, and I'll let you know what will be going down. This is gonna be big!"

A huge grin appeared on her face as she began making the necessary calls. Taking both Mario Jordan and Jermaine Hill down was proving far, far easier than she had ever imagined.

• • •

BELL DAVIS sat straight up in her bed, almost simultaneously clutching her chest as a flaring pain seared through her heart. At first she thought she might be having another heart attack, but she wasn't experiencing shortness of breath, the telltale symptom.

And then, like an epiphany of the greatest possible magnitude, she knew what was wrong. What was terribly, frighteningly wrong.

Oh, Lord, no! My baby, Lord! Save him . . .

The horrible vision came to her mind as graphically and clearly as if she had been physically walking right next to Jermaine at that moment. She had discerned the suicidal spirits that had been attacking Jermaine ever since his two best friends had been killed almost a decade earlier. And she had prayed every single day, warding off their effects through the power of intercession. But now, after all this time, were her prayers going to fail her? Had her prayers possessed any real power?

Oh, Jesus . . . She began to weep bitterly, not even

having the mind to know what else to say. She felt completely and utterly hopeless, and she wished with all her soul that she could somehow block out this image, as her deteriorating mind had done with so many others. That would have eased some of the pain, at least.

• • •

JERMAINE WAS AT A central point now atop the mountain, having navigated a narrow and difficult path unknown to many people. If one traveled it just so, one could circumvent all of the motion detectors. A city guide had told him about this secret path a few years ago, and he had just filed that little bit of information away in his mind, not knowing that it would ever prove so handy.

He had a brief thought to call Mario, but he resisted doing so. Talking with anyone right now would not be a good idea because questions might be brought up that he was neither ready nor willing to answer.

But what about Candace? I just left her there . . .

Obviously, he hadn't given much thought to the repercussions of the impulse decision to drive back here, but what did it really matter at this point? Mario would make the necessary travel arrangements to see that Candace was taken care of. And anyway, by that time Jermaine would be long gone from this world.

Yes, his feelings for Candace had surprisingly grown stronger during the course of the week, and he'd desperately wanted to demonstrate his passions to her the only way he knew how. He'd been so sure she wanted him just as much as he did her, but he'd guessed . . . wrong.

Maybe I shouldn't have pushed her . . .

But it was too late now. She was yet another closed opportunity in a life filled with so many personal disappointments.

And what about Aunt Bell? Oh, forget that crazy old woman. She's certainly forgotten about me . . .

He would make absolutely sure that nobody else had a chance to hurt or leave him. For the last time, he gazed out over the Los Angeles skyline and horizon, blanketed with the typical thin veneer of smog and haze, and then slowly closed his eyes. He visualized an endless ocean of rich, dazzling cobalt-blue color. It would be his refuge and oasis that would finally provide him the escape he so desperately sought. At last . . . he would be free! He steadied all his thoughts and energies and concentrated on taking that one, final lunge. He was leaving this hellhole, so help him—

"Mr. Jermaine Hill! Mr. Jermaine Hill! Mr. Hill!"

The loud cries came from somewhere behind him, knocking him out of his calm state of mind and causing him to turn in surprise. The whirr and clicks of a horde of cameras instantly bombarded him, as reporters and cameramen scrambled to get closer to the star speaker.

"Mr. Hill! Is it true that you and Candace Clark are secret lovers?"

"Had you purposely planned to deceive the American public by using her as the one to interview you?"

"What is your response to allegations made by a number of women who claimed you had one-night stands with them?"

"Are you worried about how these allegations might tarnish your image?"

The questions assaulted his ears like a barrage of machine gunfire, as over fifteen or so members of the press corps rushed to thrust microphones and tape recorders in his face.

What in the . . .

"Mr. Hill, is it true that you are an alcoholic?"

"Mr. Hill . . ."

"Jermaine! Jermaine Hill . . ."

The voices soon became nothing more than raucous babble to him. He didn't know how these people had managed to find him here, but if it was a show they were looking for, then he might as well give them one. For his last performance as the pawn of the ever-revolving media circus act, he'd give them something they would never forget.

He held up his hands to silence the swarming corps that were now huddled around him like teammates in a football game. Except these people were *not* on his team. They weren't even playing the same game.

"I just have one thing to say," he began slowly. The camera's red lights were on—they were rolling and recording Jermaine's every word and action. But he wasn't about to *say* anything. If actions spoke louder than words, then he was about to create a reverberation the whole wide world would soon hear. Without a word he broke to his right in a dead sprint and where the end of the cliff embraced nothing but air, he took a giant leap . . .

. . . right off the edge of the mountain.

PART II

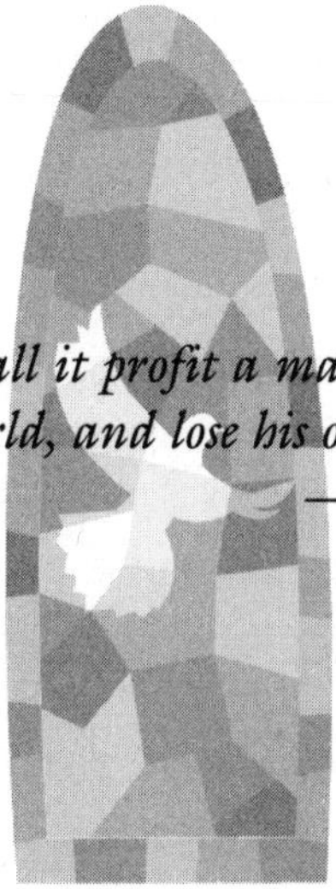

For what shall it profit a man, if he shall gain the world, and lose his own soul?

—MARK 8:36

chapter twenty-one

Four weeks later

IT CAN BE amazing and altogether humbling how mankind's plans, hurriedly pieced together, do not always produce the desired effects. Perhaps the Scottish poet Robert Burns was on to something when he wrote that "the best laid plans of mice and men often go awry." It may well have been, if Jermaine had mapped out his course of actions a bit more thoroughly—perhaps if he had gone ahead and used the .22 handgun or driven himself off a cliff somewhere—then he might have discovered whether his endless, eternal ocean was real or imagined.

But hurling himself off a point on Mount Lee had not proven to be the wisest choice for ending his life.

The attempt proved unsuccessful.

In his surprise at seeing the gathering paparazzi converge upon him like sewer rats to rotting cheese, he had misjudged the spot on the ledge where he should have jumped. He had rushed and leaped from a position a few meters to the right, landing twelve feet down in an overgrown thicket of trees and shrubbery. Had he taken off ten meters to the left, he would have plunged down a fifty-foot abyss and ended up like Peg Entwhistle in 1932. But fate can be cruel and unforgiving sometimes.

His fall into the forest thicket had shattered twenty-six bones in both legs and feet, broken four ribs, and left him with a massive concussion that would undoubtedly cause recurring headaches. All things considered in this failed suicide attempt, it could be said that he was quite fortunate to be alive. As it turned out, though, his injuries were far from his most pressing concern. As damaging as his medical diagnosis was, he would gladly have accepted that as the sole consequence for his actions. He would soon realize that fate was not alone in its ability to seem cruel and unforgiving. The media, too, were unforgiving, passing scathing judgment on him.

A subsequent investigation from the LAPD produced an unregistered .22 handgun at his Beverly Hills condominium, along with four spiral notebooks—his diary of sorts—filled with severely damaging evidence of his suicidal thought patterns. Signed statements from over a dozen Hollywood playgirls bedded by Jermaine had effectively silenced Mario Jordan's repeated arguments that his client was of "strong, moral integrity and character." For all the things Super Mario could spin, it was darn near impossible to put a positive media spin on *that* kind of behavior.

The public backlash was immediate and intense, and most of all, Jermaine's fans were *irate*. How dare this man, purporting to be America's voice of inspiration, have any sort of claim to be a leader, role model, or national icon. He was a joke, for crying out loud! A twisted, perverted joke. That was the general sentiment of a people who had grown weary of their entertainers and celebrated public figures having continual brushes with the wrong side of the law. As if having a rap sheet gave some twisted sort of "street credibility" to one's reputation. Both the media and the general public needed a scapegoat, a permanent example of these hypocritical celebrities. Especially celebrities whose opinions and ideas helped form the basis of pop culture and thinking.

• • •

JERMAINE NOW SAT STOICALLY in a wheelchair in the executive conference room, absently listening to Mario and two highly compensated lawyers map out their strategy.

"We've already lost forty-five percent of expected endorsement offers from major sponsors," Mario spoke gravely, "and we're not hearing anything more from the Fortune 100 list." He didn't have to add that these losses were indicative of a major crisis. It had been a foregone conclusion that Jermaine would royally collect from top American companies who were enlisting energetic, dynamic faces to parade before their employees. Mario, naturally, had already begun touting Jermaine as the "new voice of inspired motivationalism" to these companies, lining up unspoken agreements as quickly and quietly as he could. The dozen or so contracts were set to be signed at the start of the new year, as soon as Jermaine fulfilled his contractual obligations with KKTL. But the current, shocking turn of events had rendered Jermaine about as marketable as an audiocassette manufacturer pushing his product to the music industry. Nobody wanted anything to do with a washed-up, sex-crazed motivational speaker with suicidal tendencies.

"Naturally, it would have been in your best interests to have procured written documentation from these companies beforehand," remarked the elder of the two attorneys. Jermaine vaguely remembered his name as Stapleton or Singleton or something like that. He didn't care, of course. To him, both were just two more money-sucking leeches clinging to his money train.

"Tell me something I *don't* know, Randall," Mario retorted, openly irritated. "The money dries up in December because KKTL is stalling on a new contract, we've got no public relations spin to our latest problems, and now we've got the D.A. breathing down our necks, talking about dual weapons and solicitation charges." He dropped his head into his hands. "For chrissake, please tell me when this nightmare ends."

"That's all this is to you, isn't it?" Jermaine spoke up, his nonchalance now giving way to anger. "A stupid public relations fiasco. Your little hot commodity ain't as hot as you thought so now you're looking for the quickest, easiest out."

"Jermaine . . ." Mario began slowly, his head still in his hands, "I warned you about this, didn't I? About the women every night, about disregard for accountability—"

"Fine, fine—you *warned* me about this. Stick out your little chest about that if it makes you feel any better. But you were only telling me that to protect your bottom line. It was still all about maintaining a cash flow that kept you and your fat little friends over there satisfied."

Stapleton-Singleton-whoever opened his mouth in shock.

"Don't try and strictly make this a financial issue," Mario shot back, now looking up with an incensed expression on his face. "But since you're so eager to talk about money, before you hired me you were barely pushing thirty grand a year. Our last fiscal quarter, I netted you over eight hundred thousand big ones. In the *quarter* alone! I've been the best thing that's ever happened to you. And this is the thanks I get in return?"

"If that's what you want to call it, then yeah. I'm not saying I don't appreciate what you did, but my talent alone would have eventually gotten me the money. So maybe instead of investing in agents and lawyers, I should have been looking for some friends who would've had my back."

"There are no *friends* in this business, J. If you had wanted friends, you should have volunteered for the freakin' Peace Corps."

"Can we just relax and focus on the big picture?" asked Randall Stapleton. "There is much at stake here for all of us, and we're going to need clear minds to figure out how best to proceed."

Mario threw up his hands in disgust. "How best to proceed? And go where? There's nothing we can do to save face right now."

The other attorney spoke up. "I agree with you, Mario, but only to a point. There's too much controversy in the press to attempt any sort of campaign, sure. But if we lay low for a while, maybe have Jermaine undergo professional treatment, we could launch a comeback campaign in a few months. The public is more forgiving than you think. Look at all the chances they gave Mike Tyson and Robert Downey Jr."

"Yeah, and it's exactly *those* kinds of people that have gotten the public tired of being sympathetic."

Alex Winston shrugged. "Perhaps. Still, I vote that we place him under treatment for a while and have him come back better than ever."

"Do I get a say in this?" Jermaine cut in. "After all, it's my life you all are so *casually* talking about."

"A life that you tried to end a few weeks ago," Mario was quick to remind him. "So yeah, you can have some input but it goes without saying that you're going to need psychiatric treatment. Placing you somewhere like Atascadero might be the only thing that keeps the D.A. off our backs."

"Psychiatric treatment? What is this, *One Flew over the Cuckoo's Nest*? You guys think I'm crazy or something?"

A lengthy pause ensued. Jermaine could read between the lines.

"Jermaine, you attempted suicide. Apparently, there are some irregularities in your mental capacities that should be professionally dealt with," offered Randall, with a little more condescension than Jermaine could presently stomach.

"My mental capacities are just fine, for your information. If anything, I'm tired of always having my decisions made by people who know absolutely nothing about me."

Mario sighed. "Oh, give it a rest, J. This is about the only positive thing we can do here. Honesty is the best policy, right? You go public admitting you have a problem and are currently seeking help, and I guarantee you the people will eat that stuff up. I can picture you on *Oprah*, *The View*, hitting all the tear-jerker shows like that."

Jermaine rolled his eyes. *Forever spinning, aren't you Mario?*

• • •

THE LIGHTS IN THE sunroom were off and the shades on all the windows were tightly drawn. Candace didn't even have any music playing at the moment—she simply lay curled up on her sofa, staring at nothing in particular. She didn't know how long she had been lying here, just that she savored the present solitary quietness. Craved it, in fact. Because after *StarWatch News* had broken their story about an alleged romantic relationship between her and Jermaine, Candace had suddenly and unexpectedly been thrust into the probing glare of a national spotlight. Her face had been splashed on the front pages of newspapers and tabloids countrywide. And her now-infamous kiss with Jermaine on Venice Beach was getting more exposure than a top music video in heavy MTV rotation. Reporters had camped out on her street for days seeking to catch a glimpse of her through a window, rendering her a virtual prisoner in her own home.

A low blow had also been struck when a handful of literary colleagues began appearing on the prime-time interview shows, capitalizing on the scandal to try to damage her character even more. They knew Candace Clark couldn't be the perfect success story, they had all gloated. Little Miss Perfect writer who seemingly had everything handed to her on a polished silver platter.

Though she had refused to dwell on it much before all this happened, Candace was well aware that her quick rise to success had created quite a few personal enemies—haters who couldn't bear to see a younger, less seasoned writer reap awards that they felt should have gone to someone with more experience. But because her writing was always top-notch, people were usually limited in the amount of negative things they could say. When you're really good at something, people don't have to like you but they've certainly got to respect you. That's what she had always thought, anyway.

But rumors of a steamy relationship between her and Jermaine Hill had provided more than enough darts for this jealous peanut gallery to throw, a gallery that had come to include Tasha, of all people. That had hurt Candace the most—that her best friend would think so little of her as to agree with her accusers.

"Well, you never told me you were even doing the interview," Tasha had argued. "So how am I supposed to believe anything else you say about him?" Tasha had then proceeded to give Candace a fit of Motown diva-like proportions.

"Did you sleep with him?" she had asked.

Candace's slight hesitation upon hearing that question had prompted a burst of hysterical tears to erupt from Tasha like a black Niagara Falls. The tears were followed up by a classic, weave-whipping, finger-snapping, neck-twisting exit from her house after Candace remained silent and unable to answer the question. For what was she supposed to say? *Technically*, she and Jermaine hadn't gone that far, but she still had admittedly crossed the line in her journalistic ethics.

If she were honest with herself, deep down she would have to admit harboring some feelings for the man. Feelings for a man the media had been labeling as crazy—why else would he have written hundreds of suicide plots in his personal diary?

But in all the time she had spent with him, she had not observed such tendencies in this man. Sure, it had only been for one week, since Jermaine's departure had cut her interview short, but she had always thought herself an excellent judge of character. So in spite of the overwhelming evidence claiming otherwise, she still chose to see him as a perceptive, intelligent black man with a sensitive side that came out when gently motivated. How rare a find was *that*? Outrageously, though, her choice to view him as such was the singular reason her good name was being wrongly tarnished and looked down upon like a modern-day Hester Prynne.

"But I haven't done anything wrong!" Her mind screamed. She certainly didn't think she deserved this scarlet letter. But the media, naturally, would be relentless in promoting this story because it had wonderful shock value. This scandal would continue to dominate

the headlines until another titillating and jaw-dropping event happened to push it to the "yesterday's news" pile. That was the way the media worked—she knew that all too well.

You're just going to have to deal with this, girl . . .

It would have been nice to have a strong support group to help her cope with everything, but a major sacrifice Candace had made along her career's fast track to success had been the heavy cost of maintaining relationships. She had been forced to determine what she valued the most—her writing, social life, family and friends—and in the end, she had decided to follow her heart. So though she had more acquaintances than she could possibly keep track of, she had no real friends besides Tasha and her mother, Analee. Analee, of course, was gone. And Tasha was currently trippin'. So in her darkest hour, at a time when there should have been a shoulder for her to cry on, she was all alone.

"God, help me . . ." she softly whispered to the dark, empty room. Though she believed in God, it had been a long time since she had last talked to Him. Perhaps now was a good time to firm up that fading line of communication.

chapter twenty-two

MYRA HAD LIVED long enough to learn how to count her blessings, no matter how small they sometimes seemed. But when the doubly shocking scandal stories were released (Jermaine and Candace's secret relationship and then Jermaine's suicide attempt), Myra had suffered an epic faith-crisis, not only in God, but in herself to navigate wisely through this predicament. She was clueless as to how *Song of Solomon* could recover, financially and in moral standing, from a too-close-to-home scandal that had rocked them at the worst possible time. But, as Xavier continually reminded her, sometimes God allows trying situations to beset His children only so their faith might be strengthened and established.

Though the magazine suffered some initial attacks to reputation and credibility, the majority of the media analysts chose not to implicate the publication in the larger scandal as a whole. This was undoubtedly due to the magazine's publicized mission statement, which firmly adhered to a standard of Christian principles in entertaining and providing a social forum for the nation. Besides, Candace really had no binding ties to the magazine except for the lone contract to write the one story. A story that still turned out to be quite good, considering the interview was cut short by a week. Fortunately for *Song of Solomon*, the public demand still remained high due to the sudden spike of interest in Jermaine's private life. Now, the nation was clamoring to know if Candace was really as close to Jermaine as rumor would suggest. Or if Jermaine was really as deranged as everyone thought. And they were counting on Candace's exclusive story to give them added details and first-person insight. Day by day and week by passing week, the media feeding frenzy made this story top priority.

The past few days, Myra had tried calling Candace, but the young writer had apparently taken her phone off the hook. Not that Myra could blame her for doing that—she felt so sorry for what that girl was now being forced to go through. It seemed such a shame to Myra that the media would be falling over themselves trying to expose any speck of dirt they could on these two promising, young black role models. So what if Jermaine and Candace were not as perfect and pristine as everyone thought? Nowadays, *who* was? Myra sincerely believed this was more reason to encourage people to look to her Savior for a true example to pattern life after. Because people were imperfect and would always let you down, no matter how gifted, talented, or wonderful they appeared. It had taken years of disappointing relationships for Myra to understand that in the search for human role models, she'd never find any if her measuring stick was perfection. For the best that people can be is not perfect, merely *forgiven.* True human role models are the ones who ultimately choose God's grace to work in their sinful lives. And then, like a butterfly bursting forth from its cocoon, they become transformed into new creations reflecting His image and divine character.

It was her heartfelt prayer that both Jermaine and Candace would come to understand this as well, she hoped before it was too late—before the media thoroughly and completely robbed them of their future hopes and dreams, of their God-given gifts and abilities to *inspire* others.

• • •

IT HAD BECOME official, much to Mario Jordan's great relief. Jermaine was ordered to undergo three months of thoroughly rigorous treatment at Atascadero, and the D.A.'s office agreed not to press charges against him. The renowned facility for mental health problems located roughly halfway between Los Angeles and San Francisco was a perfect refuge for Jermaine to heal, rest, and most important remain sheltered from the media. Mario had been forced to immediately cancel the remaining events on Jermaine's itinerary and attempt an assortment of damage-control maneuvers that might swing some public sympathy toward his client. He envisioned Jermaine emerging from this setback with an even larger following—showing America and the world that you could be great and still have flaws. You could be talented but still struggle with troubling inner issues. Such a personal, human touch would work in their favor, Mario thought. And with a little time and patience, he could see the endorsements and money flowing freely once again in their direction.

Everything would be alright, he reassured himself as he sat at his desk, poring over a new stack of audition announcements he was currently funneling to some of his other clients. Forever on the move, he was constantly lining up his diverse client list with the most promising movies and commercials that show business had to offer. He was a master at what he did, negotiating deal after lucrative deal and landing more contracts than should be legally permissible. But as good as he was in this aspect of the business, Mario's personal pride shone the brightest when he was able to spin a news story any which way he desired. Subtly persuading public opinion to see things as you wanted it to—well, that took a level of skill that only a select few possessed. And fewer still had the unmitigated audacity to even attempt. But the "Super" in his nickname was neither an exaggeration nor a crude reference to some once-popular video game. No, he truly believed he could accomplish super feats in his lifetime—that he would go down as a legend in the art of negotiating and spin control.

So what if his number one client presently had more image problems than an Elizabeth Taylor weekend forum on how to make loving marriages last. Mario was by no means new to this game. The spotlight was on him and he relished every moment of it. And when this little crisis subsided, Mario was betting that his client would *still* be the most famous, most listened to motivational speaker in the country.

chapter twenty-three

FROM THE MOMENT Jermaine was placed inside the all-male mental health facility, he felt he had personally sunk to one of the lowest levels in his life. It was like Aunt Bell's taking him out of that drug-infested apartment in Brooklyn when he was three—crying and screaming and wondering why Pops and Mom couldn't come along as well. It was like his receiving the message that Ronny and Eric had been tragically killed when a drunk driver had veered into their lane, forever erasing for Jermaine the last vestiges of friendship and brotherhood he had ever known. So now, here he was—stripped of his acclaim and wealth—merely another patient inside the walls of Atascadero State Hospital.

Should've killed myself . . . what kind of fool can't even kill himself right?

His legs remained indefinitely unusable, and the harsh reality that he needed someone to help him get out of bed, clothe him, and otherwise take care of him was utterly humiliating. A small comfort had been the assurance that his stay here would not be for long if he was cooperative and agreed to participate in all therapy sessions. But in Jermaine's pitiful mind-set, that was the equivalent of petting a small puppy on the head and promising it some doggie biscuits if it behaved while left home alone for the weekend.

"And it shall come to pass, that the Lord God Almighty shall rain down fire and brimstone upon the nations who do not . . ."

The old, crazy man in the room next to Jermaine's had been ranting for over an hour with his religious nonsense, and Jermaine was now thoroughly sickened. Wearily, he rolled his wheelchair into the narrow hallway and stopped at the old man's door.

"The Lord shall—"

"Hey! Hey, old man," Jermaine cut in as he entered the man's room. "How 'bout some peace and quiet, huh? Why don't you give everybody around here a little rest?"

Ambrose stopped his pacing and, with a curious expression on his face, looked at the visitor who had dared to interrupt him. "A little rest, you say? My son, the Word of God declares there *is* no rest for the wicked. For the unrighteous—"

"Yeah, yeah. And Jesus is coming back tomorrow. I've heard all that before, so don't waste any more breath on account of me."

"Oh, I am not wasting my breath," Ambrose replied, shaking his head. "Not with you, my son. For the Lord God has sent you here just so you could listen to the words of truth I speak."

"That right?" Jermaine asked, thinking it quite harmless to play along for a minute. This was exactly the kind of guy he expected to find in a state hospital. *Let's see what you're made of, old man* . . . "You mean to tell me that God—in His busy schedule between keeping the planets all aligned and, oh I don't know, keeping the sun from burning the earth and crazy dictators from starting the next world war—*actually* put all that more important stuff on hold and interrupted my life to get me here to listen to your crazy talk?"

Ambrose raised an eyebrow. "My son, if you were not so sarcastic, perhaps you might have realized the prophetic vein in which you just spoke."

Jermaine held out his hands. "First off, let's cool it with the whole *my son* thing, alright? This ain't *The Godfather*, Don Corleone. And second, why don't you just take a look around at where you are? You're in a mental hospital, man! Nobody's taking what you have to say seriously."

With tightly pursed lips, Ambrose forced a thin smile and proceeded to sit down in a folding chair underneath the room's lone window. "I do suppose, Mr. Jermaine Hill, that you know a little about what it means to have people take your words seriously."

Jermaine couldn't help his surprised expression. "How do you know my name?" he demanded.

Ambrose calmly shrugged. "You are, as they say, a celebrity. In my estimation, I would think it more a surprise if I *did not* know your name."

Visibly taken aback, Jermaine struggled to keep his demeanor calm. He had not expected such a candid response from the man. "Oh. Well, well . . ." He didn't quite know what to say.

"My name is Ambrose Rivers," the old man said,

"pleased to meet you. No, no—you don't have to get up." He heartily laughed at his own humor, a throaty cackle that seemed to go on and on. "Perhaps you would like me to explain why I speak so *loud*?"

"No. No, I don't care why you think you need to be loud, to tell you the truth. Didn't you hear what I said? Nobody around here cares about what you have to say."

"Hmm . . ." Ambrose rubbed his eyes for a second. "Might I ask you a question, Mr. Hill?"

Jermaine shrugged, which in his present wheelchair-bound state, didn't quite give off the same arrogance he was hoping for.

"Did you care whether or not people listened to what *you* had to say?"

"Actually, most of the time I didn't care what anyone thought. But I wasn't getting anything but praise and adoration from my fans, anyway. So obviously, they *were* listening to me."

"Listening and hearing are two quite different things, my son. Tell me, were you advising them with words of wisdom?"

"I told them what they wanted to hear. It's just human nature to want to feel good about yourselves, to want somebody to pat you on the back and tell you to reach for the sky and all that."

Ambrose shook his head. "Telling people what they want to hear is not a true definition of wisdom. For the Bible says that the Lord Himself gives wisdom; from His mouth comes knowledge and understanding."

Jermaine rolled his eyes, feeling a bit sorry for the man, whose wrinkly old brain was obviously stuck in his tired, outdated scriptures. "Don't you know it's those kind of statements that keep making people like *you* unpopular? No wonder people think you're crazy. You and every other Bible-totin', Scripture-quotin' preacher who thinks he's got all the answers."

Ambrose seemed not to be outwardly daunted by the accusation. "Ah, but the fact that we, as a human race, *have* these sorts of questions surely suggests that somebody *should* have the answers, yes? And who should that somebody be?"

The question was rhetorical, but Jermaine somehow had the feeling that the old man was seeking a response.

"Apparently, a lot of people are under the impression that *you* have them," Ambrose added.

Jermaine was silent, once more having nothing to say.

• • •

THE LAST TIME Candace had set foot in Longview, Texas, she had been a little girl, just eleven years old. She remembered that she had come here then to attend her grandmother's funeral—her father's mother, whom she hadn't been very close to. Not only had it been her first time to view someone who had passed away (Daddy, she looks like she's sleeping!), but it had also been her first experience of life on a farm. And those unpleasant, eye-opening few days had probably been as good a reason as any why she had not since been back to her father's hometown.

Analee had suggested she and Candace stay in a hotel during that weekend—giving Harold some necessary time and space to grieve his mother's passing with the rest of the Clark family.

"No—we *all* are family," Harold had firmly responded, even though he knew his brothers and sisters had never really approved of his high-maintenance, upper-class wife. "And we *all* are going to stay on my mother's farm during this time of bereavement."

It wasn't a large farm, just a few acres, but there had been more chickens, cows, and pigs than a young Candace could tolerate. And when one of the rambunctious, squealing little pigs had gotten loose and chased after her, it left her severely traumatized at the sight of pigs for years afterward. To this day, she still could not fully enjoy the taste of bacon.

She had come back to Longview now, almost in a sense of desperation. For where else could she go? To whom else could she turn? Her fierce independence, inherited from her mother, had always been a source of great strength for her. She took great personal pride in the fact that she had traveled all around the world by her twentieth birthday, had her features published to glowing critical acclaim, and even had her book enjoy a stint on the *New York Times* best-seller list. And of course the Pulitzer was still out there, just beyond her grasp but squarely within the reach of someone so talented, headstrong, and ambitious. But her independence was also a masquerade; behind it she hid weakness. Because that dominating little character trait rendered her virtually all alone at a time when she needed comforting the most.

"Sweetheart, you doing okay this morning?" Harold walked in the kitchen and gave his daughter a hug as she stood at the stove, fixing an omelet. "I checked in on you last night and you were tossin' and turnin' something good."

"I'm fine, Daddy. And you don't have to check on me—I'm not so little anymore."

Harold gave a big *humph* as he sat down at the table and spread out his *Longview News-Journal* to go along with his regular cup of coffee. "You're gon' always be my little girl, and I'll check in on you every night if I want to, even when you get to be as old as I am."

"Daddy!" She thought about throwing a dishrag at him. Nevertheless, she was elated at the ease with which they now seemed to be conversing.

Harold playfully made a show of sniffing the air. "Candi, is you tryin' to *cook* over there? Great smoogly-woogly, I didn't think I would ever live to see the day you would be back here, and cooking breakfast no less. Your mother, God bless her heart, didn't even do *that*!"

"Relax, Daddy. I'm just making some omelets. And a word of free advice for you—normal and intelligent people don't say phrases like *great smoogly-woogly.*"

"I's got a college degree just like you, young lady," he said between sips of coffee.

"Then that proves my point about small towns—you've been back *here* too long," came Candace's quick reply, sending her into a fit of laughter.

• • •

"SO, SWEETHEART, you and that Jermaine Hill, there was . . . um, there was nothing going on between you two?" Candace and her father were sitting on the expansive porch, enjoying cool glasses of iced tea and watching the occasional car roll past them on the dirt road. Oddly enough, to Candace's normal jet-setting life, the huge contrast of Longview's slower pace was refreshing.

She fingered the cool drops of condensation forming on the sides of the Mason jar that was currently posing as a drinking glass. Then again, out here these *were* the regular drinking glasses. "No, there wasn't anything going on . . ."

"I see. So—"

" . . . yet."

"Yet?" Harold looked at her with a questioning fatherly glance.

"Well, I . . . I was starting to have feelings for him. And I think he felt the same way about me. Or maybe not. I . . . I don't know. I guess it used to be easier talking about this with Mom than you . . ."

"I understand, Candi. You don't have to, if you don't . . . you know, if you don't want to . . ."

Candace sighed. "I've just had the worst luck with men in the past few years. It's getting harder to read the signals anymore. I thought Jermaine liked me, but . . . but it wasn't even supposed to be like that between the two of us, you know? I was on assignment, for goodness sakes!"

"He was that charming, then?"

"No, not at first. He had this wall up, you know? And I did my best to get past that wall because I wanted to really show everyone a side of him that no one else knew."

"Obviously, he really *did* have a side to him that nobody else knew."

Candace shrugged, biting back the words she wanted to say. *But Jermaine wasn't the crazy person everybody was making him out to be!*

"You know, sweetheart, I've had a lot of time to pray and think about things since I moved back here. Since your mother . . ." he let the sentence drift. "Well, anyway . . . praying has really been helping me, you know? Talking to God about the issues in my life. Reading His Word. The kind of things instilled in me by my own father that I just sort of drifted away from."

He reached over and patted his daughter's hand. "And if it wasn't for that spiritual reconnection, I don't think I would be able to deal with life at all." He was silent for several minutes. Then he looked at Candace and added, "You know, your mother used to pray every night before she went to sleep. Never said much too loud, but I saw her lips moving. And sometimes she would be crying quietly, trying not to wake me up. Did you know she prayed faithfully like that every night?"

Candace blinked away some tears trying their best to roll down her face. There would probably always be things she never knew about her mother. "No, I . . . no. I didn't know that."

chapter twenty-four

AMBROSE CONTINUED TO methodically pace the length of floor in his room, praying in a hushed voice but losing none of the fervor as when he spoke at a loud volume. His prayers, entire quotations of biblical scriptures as they mostly were, rolled off his tongue with the smoothness of butter melting on a hot country griddle.

"There is a spirit in man, and the inspiration of the Almighty giveth them understanding . . . oh Lord, let Your light shine upon the blinded eyes of Jermaine, the light of the glorious gospel of Christ that opens the eyes of the spiritually blind . . . and the treasure that is in Jermaine—the excellency of its power comes from You, my Lord. So draw him to You with loving kindness and let him understand that his golden voice has been anointed only to speak Your words of inspiration . . . open his eyes, my Lord. Open his eyes . . ."

Ambrose had not slept in three days, so intense was the mandate laid upon him to pray for this young man's soul. He was equally humbled, yet honored to be chosen as a chief intercessor for Jermaine—a man who yet remained unaware of the highly precious gift he possessed. It was not merely an oratory gift; many people had been blessed with the ability to speak eloquently and make harmony from the spoken word. But Ambrose sensed Jermaine's gift was far more substantial than that.

But it could be so much more . . . he could be much more . . .

"Lord, let him be more . . . Let him speak for You . . ."

• • •

THE DREAM WAS coming back in Jermaine's mind, more vivid now than ever. And it wasn't just any dream, it was the same recurring nightmare that had plagued him since his college years. In the dream, Jermaine was in front of a huge crowd in the cavernous Pasadena Rose Bowl. He was the celebrated speaker of the hour, and as he sat on the stage that had been erected along the midfield line, he could sense the palpable excitement and expectation from the stirring crowd.

"Jeeer-maainne! Jeeer-maainne!" they exuberantly cried out, over a hundred thousand voices unified to form one thunderous roar. All of them were anxiously waiting to hear the man with the golden voice.

When his moment had finally arrived, he stood tall and proud and strode to the podium, pausing at length to bask in the unconditional acceptance of his adoring fans. It was a powerful adrenaline rush normally experienced by only a handful of rock stars or popular presidential nominees—hearing your name ceremoniously chanted over and over until such adulation approaches the status of worship.

Jermaine had absorbed all of this with great pride—the love, admiration, and blind faith the crowd was vesting in him to excite and inspire them about life. With his trademark winning smile, he raised his hands and edged closer to the microphones. Then he opened his mouth—

—and . . . *nothing* came . . . out.

Momentarily stunned, he had tried clearing his throat. Wetting his lips. But to his horror, there was to be no sound proceeding from his voice box. Suddenly and quite shockingly, he had been rendered completely mute. The overflowing crowd, which moments before had been so vociferously alive, had since quieted down in preparation for hearing their beloved speaker. But as Jermaine continued to stand there, feeling more and more vulnerable with each passing second, confused murmurs now began rippling throughout the stadium.

What was going on here?

Beads of sweat popped out all along Jermaine's forehead as his face took on a panicked, "deer caught in the headlights" expression. There was no place for him to hide, and no reasonable action he could presently take. For everyone was there solely to hear *him.* He had been brought to the apex of fame and power because of his vocal gift to motivate the masses. But without the ability and wherewithal to even *make a noise* with his mouth, what good was he? Without the one thing that had defined him and garnered him the esteem and reverence of millions, *who* was he?

He was lost was what he was. Pitifully and utterly . . .

lost. At this point in the dream, as always, it became harder for him to breathe. As he began to labor mightily for each breath, his knees started to wobble and buckle. The last thought before he would awake to sweat-soaked sheets was how hard it had been for him to breathe. To *breathe*!

Mercifully jolted from his nightmare, Jermaine rolled over on his right side in the small bed, holding his head in the cup of his hands and gulping for each lungful of air. The ringing in his ears and in the center of his skull was not yet migraine level, but he found no comfort in that small detail. As he continued to lie there on the bed, slowly regaining his breath, two distinct fears began to rise strongly within him. For not only was he afraid of drifting back to sleep and reliving that traumatic experience, but he also was fearful of remaining awake in a reality not so far removed from that nightmare.

chapter twenty-five

IT WAS ALMOST time, now. Bell could sense it, feel it. And in many ways, the old woman of faith embraced the divine transition. While most people feared death because of the questions of the unknown, Bell's soul was anchored. Her heart was ready. With eyes made blurry by slow, streaming tears, she read once again in her large-print Bible the stirring words of the apostle Paul.

"I have fought the good fight, I have finished the race, I have kept the faith . . ."

She had not traveled to a lot of places in her life, earned a whole lot of money, or anything else that people would consider having lived a successful life. But she had worked her job honestly and fairly. And she had raised Jermaine like he was her son. Raised him *as her son.*

I've kept the faith, Jesus. I've kept the faith . . .

She was ready for her heavenly reward, but she still had the faith to believe there was a reward for her right now, as well. The fact that Jermaine had not died when he fell off that cliff encouraged her that there was still a chance. There was still hope for her son. And that would be her earthly reward—to see Jermaine saved and using his gift for the glory of God.

I've kept the faith . . .

• • •

THE NEXT FEW DAYS dragged by at an agonizingly slow crawl for him, made even worse because of his inability to sleep at night. His nightmare still haunted him—exploding with terror back into his consciousness every time he closed his eyes for any significant length of time. And with that nightmare came old, unresolved feelings of worthlessness because he was reminded of what might happen if his ability to speak was taken away.

But it's just a dream . . . I'm still able to talk . . .

Yes, he still had the ability to talk. But what good was using his mouth to motivate others if he still remained unable to eradicate the depression weighing down his own soul?

"I know about your dreams, Jermaine." At the sound of the interrupting voice, Jermaine rolled his wheelchair around to find Ambrose leaning against his opened door.

The nerve of this crazy old man . . . "What?"

"I know about the dreams you've been having for quite some time now."

"Oh, yeah? Everybody has dreams, old man."

Ambrose shrugged and took a few cautious steps inside the room. "But you and I both know that it is only one dream, and it is quite *unlike* the sorts of dreams everybody else has." He then proceeded to describe it in great detail—right down to the stunned silence of the thousands of spectators and Jermaine's gasping for breath on wobbling, buckling knees. When he finished with the description he sat down on the bed, his face now eye level with Jermaine's.

"Did you know that God sometimes speaks to us in dreams?"

Jermaine cleared his throat, forcing himself to look away from the man's penetrating eyes. It was extremely unnerving—like Ambrose was staring right into the innermost depths of his heart. "Always bringing up God, aren't you? Well here's a news flash, Ambrose. People have dreams all the time. It's completely natural. I don't think that it means God is trying to say something to me."

"But you know, the Lord spoke to many people in the Bible through dreams. Abraham, Jacob, Solomon, just to name a few. I am merely suggesting that God may be trying to arrest your attention at a time when you have no other choice but to listen—when you are asleep. Tell me something. Have you always wanted to be a . . . a . . . what is the correct term?"

"A motivational speaker."

"Yes, yes—a motivational speaker. You have always wanted to be one?"

Jermaine shrugged, gradually beginning to feel his defensive walls slowly coming down. Maybe it was due to the still-shocking reality that he was currently in a mental hospital, or because the only other people he might have occasion to open up to were on his own payroll, making them always partial to him. But this man seemingly had nothing to gain by what Jermaine told him.

"I don't know. I . . . guess. I mean, I've always been able to connect with people through my speaking. Ever since I was a little kid. And my Aunt Bell . . ."

Am I really saying all this?

" . . . my Aunt Bell, she used to take me around with her on the weekends and let me talk to groups of elderly people in nursing homes. She . . . uh, she used to volunteer at those kinds of places all the time." He could not believe he was freely unloading all of this personal history, but then again what did he have to lose? What did it matter anymore, really?

"At first, I used to hate going. But after I started talking to them—you should've seen how their faces just lit up like firecrackers on the Fourth of July . . . I got hooked, I guess. So little by little, I started doing all sorts of things for the community, churches, schools—you name it. I was a little legend all around Baltimore. Practically had my own speaking business before I even graduated high school."

"It is evident that your whole life has been shaped around your speaking. I have to tell you, though—what you *do* is not who you *are*, my son. I know we try to combine those two areas, but it does not work that way. Just because you are gifted in a particular area does not mean that such a talent will define every aspect of your life. And in your case, I am sad to tell you, though you are an inspirational speaker, you seem not to know what inspiration truly is."

Jermaine's eyes narrowed in slight irritation, but for some reason he did not swiftly respond with a sarcastic remark. Something about the old man's gentle rebuke reminded him of how his Aunt Bell used to talk to him. Stern love. Tough love.

"Would you care to know what inspiration really is?"

Almost a minute passed before Jermaine, almost imperceptibly, nodded.

Ambrose looked to the ceiling for a moment. When he finally spoke, his voice was trembling ever so slightly. "There is a spirit in man . . . and the inspiration of the Almighty giveth them understanding. That is from the book of Job, my son." He paused before continuing. "So you see, there is a spirit within us breathed from God Himself that produces a yearning for a greater understanding of life. It is the breath of God living inside every human being that makes us long to witness the extraordinary, yes, even the supernatural. It is the breath of God that makes us long to live abundant, purpose-filled and joyful lives. For God breathed into us the breath of life and caused us to become living souls. Literally, that is what the word *inspire* means—*to breathe in*. Did you know that?"

Jermaine shook his head.

"The One who breathed into us and caused us to become living souls . . . He is the only one who can truly . . . inspire us."

chapter twenty-six

FOUR CURRENT ARTICLES from prominent national newspapers lay strewn across Mario Jordan's desk, each one providing a victory of sorts for the agent. His client had now been receiving treatment at Atascadero for a month, and in the all-important public opinion polls, the first signs of positive change were beginning to emerge.

Mercifully taken off the front page at last (a place reserved for the more-pressing war against terrorism and the resulting partisan politicking), the news of the country's former number one motivational speaker now centered around the reputed progress of his psychiatric treatments. The latest rumors on the Los Angeles grapevine were all reporting Jermaine to be responding wonderfully to his therapy. And in Mario's opinion, the best news of all was that Chantal Dixon and *StarWatch News* were finally relenting in their all-out attack to defame the name of both himself and Jermaine. It had been a crushing and humiliating beating, to be sure, but Mario knew that it would not last forever. Because as Chantal's stock began to rise—she was currently entertaining offers from the networks—a dynamic was actually beginning to work in Mario's favor. For when Chantal got hired on by the big-leaguers, she would have less and less time for following up on personal vendettas. Everything was brilliantly going according to plan.

"Ah, the powers of a master spin doctor," he thought to himself as he prepared to make several calls to the producers of key daytime talk shows. Upon Jermaine's now sooner-than-expected release, Mario was making sure he engineered a perfectly constructed itinerary designed to engender maximum public sympathy. In no time at all, his client would once again be the most visible and sought-after speaker on the circuit. The man with the golden voice would again be the best—better than the best in fact, because now Jermaine would have the added advantage of the comeback factor. Everyone loved seeing heroes make a comeback.

• • •

CANDACE HAD NOT been to church in what seemed like ages. And as she parked her car in the lot of the large non-denominational church she had once called home during her college years at Rice, she was suddenly overcome with regret. How long had it been since she had been here last?

Too, too long . . .

She had used, of course, the convenient excuses of always being too busy to have time to go to church. After all, she was on the fast track for the Pulitzer, wasn't she? And after such a prestigious award was in her coffers perhaps she would enjoy a few writing fellowships abroad, guest lecturing at universities worldwide. She could dreamily and realistically envision herself as a younger version of Maya Angelou.

Career, career, career . . . that tunnel-vision line of thinking had cost her one relationship after the other, but she hadn't cared at the time. Amazing how success had blinded her to the things and people that mattered most.

Upon entering the sanctuary, Candace was greeted warmly and lovingly by numerous church members radiating an unconditional love and acceptance that she had almost forgotten existed. Here, she did not have to wear her ultra-feminine, successful businesswoman façade. She could simply be Candace Clark—Harold and Analee's little wide-eyed, loving girl. What a relief that was!

Oh, it feels so good to be back . . .

She found herself easily giving over to the Spirit as the service began, opening in radical praise and worship with the music of Fred Hammond's "Let the Praise Begin." And though Candace did not know any of the congregants seated around her, within minutes she found herself clapping and dancing right along with them—like she'd known them for years.

As the song approached its popular chorus, the whole church sang out in wonderful unison and harmony. And Candace was certainly ready for both her blessing and her miracle. Her heart was now softened, due to an increase in her prayers over the last few weeks. She directly attributed her praying to the media's bloodthirsty rush to tarnish her name and reputation. When she was humbled and broken, it had seemed as though the only place she could find solace and comfort was on her knees in prayer. Prayer to the God whom her own daddy was seeking yet again. To the God that her mother Analee had communed with every night before she had lain down to rest.

And this God—her heavenly Father who had become the one source of comfort and refuge for Candace during the most difficult time in her life—drew His arms around her and tenderly welcomed her back to Him. Back to His unconditional and forgiving love.

chapter twenty-seven

THE NIGHTMARE WAS beginning to change. At the point where he normally would begin gasping for breath and would seem about to collapse on the stage, for the first time Jermaine was now hearing a loud voice emanating from the crowd.

"And the Lord God formed man of the dust of the ground, and breathed into his nostrils the breath of life; and man became a living being."

Jermaine awoke to sweat-soaked sheets again as the dream abruptly ended, but instead of feeling the usual gripping fear, he was filled with . . . with a strange, almost unnatural sense of peace.

The breath of life . . . inspire . . . a living being . . .

There was enough strength in his lower body and legs for him to now raise himself out of the bed. With great effort he did so, carefully lowering himself into the wheelchair. Seconds later he was at Ambrose's room, knocking softly on the door. Exactly *why* he was there he did not know, only that he felt like talking with someone. And he knew Ambrose didn't sleep at night—for all the time Jermaine had been here, the man had stayed up every night pacing the floor and reciting his scriptures.

At the sight of Jermaine, Ambrose halted his pacing, but he seemed not surprised at all to see his celebrity hallmate. In fact, if Jermaine hadn't known any better, it was almost as if Ambrose had expected this visit.

"Couldn't sleep, Jermaine?"

Jermaine wearily nodded. "I'm going crazy with this nightmare. I've forgotten what it ever felt like to have a good night's sleep."

Ambrose sat down on his bed. "I can relate to that. Though I feel my own restlessness is purely by choice, unlike yours. Still I believe I can help. I know a way to make you completely free of the hold this obviously has on you."

Jermaine studied the old man for a moment. It was hard to think of the guy as anything but crazy (they *were* in a state hospital, after all), but sometimes it actually seemed as if he knew exactly what he was talking about. And Jermaine desperately needed—craved, even—to just once be able to lay down and enjoy the simple pleasure of a good rest.

What have I got to lose? "Let me get this straight. You're saying you can take away the nightmares I've been having?"

"As I have already told you, God Himself may be just trying to arrest your attention through these dreams. Their purpose may be similar to that of Moses' burning bush."

"Moses' *what*?"

The old man chuckled. "Just a biblical example. My point is, after you take the time to listen to what God is saying to you, there will be no need for terrorizing dreams to keep you awake."

Jermaine pondered that statement for a moment. "I gotta admit that in a weird, religious sort of way, your suggestion actually makes sense." He rolled farther into the room, closer to Ambrose. "So what do I have to do?"

"Nothing, really. Just let me pray for you."

"Bet you've been waiting to do that ever since I got here," Jermaine said with a nervous laugh. "Just don't put a curse on me, preacher man."

Ambrose smiled. "Actually, I'm going to do the opposite and speak forth the blessings to come over your life." He stood up and walked over to the wheelchair, placing his hand on the star speaker's forehead.

Jermaine felt like he should close his eyes or something. *When was the last time I've done this?* He vaguely remembered Aunt Bell making one of her tear-jerking, highly emotional pleas to God over him when he had graduated from Howard and made the cross-country move to Los Angeles. But that had been years ago.

"My Father and my God," Ambrose began, "it is an honor to come before You once again. This time I am making petition on behalf of someone I know You have been longing to establish a relationship with. For You have given this man a great gift—an ability to motivate the hearts and minds of people all across the world. But the greater gift still lies beyond his understanding. So now, Lord, I simply ask that You reveal that greater gift unto Him. Soften his heart, dear Father, and breathe into him Your abundant life. Reveal unto him such holy, divine inspiration that will transform not only him, but the lives of millions of others who will listen to the words he speaks. Let Your purpose for his life come to pass. Inspire him, my Father, as only You can. And when he is converted, allow his testimony to impact the nations for Your glory! In Jesus' name, amen."

Jermaine blinked a couple of times, slightly confused. "Th-that's it? But you didn't even mention the dream I've been having. I didn't need to hear that *soften his heart* stuff and *inspire him, dear Father* and all that. I hate to tell you this, old man, but you may have just wasted your time."

"Oh no, no. Communing with the Father is anything but a waste of time, my son. I may be locked up here in this hospital, but let me tell you something—my prayers *reach* Heaven, Jermaine."

"Okay. Whatever. Are we done here?"

Ambrose nodded. "Yes. For the moment, we are done."

"You still holding to your theory that my nightmares are over?"

"I am. And it is not just a theory. When you return to your room and fall back asleep, you will discover exactly just what I am talking about. Have faith, Jermaine."

Jermaine highly doubted that he would have faith, but if anything he hoped the old man's crazy religion, like a wish granted from a genie, was at least good for an uneventful and undisturbed night's rest.

• • •

THE DREAM CREPT back into his mind yet again while he slept. But for the first time ever, the jam-packed crowd was not wildly and raucously chanting his name. Instead, they remained in their seats, respectfully creating a hushed-like anticipation that actually seemed greater in multiplied effect than if they had been screaming at the top of their lungs. And for a long while Jermaine sat, observing and thoroughly absorbing the entire atmosphere. Then with not so much as the faintest tremor in his knees, he stood and made his way to the podium at center stage. Looking out among the sea of faces he paused for a few seconds, experiencing the adrenaline surge he always felt just before he was to publicly speak. But this time, the rush felt infinitely greater than he had ever remembered. A deluge of unbridled energy passed through his very being, so amazingly dazzling that for a moment he thought he might pass out from the sheer ecstasy.

"This, Jermaine Hill, is true joy unspeakable and full of glory . . ."

What! Where had that voice come from? Its firm, yet still soothing tone was tremendously comforting, like the sound of many rushing waters. Like the voice of a . . . well, like the voice of a . . . *father*. Straining to hear the words once more he was, to his disappointment, met with absolute silence. He opened his mouth then, not knowing if he would even be able to speak and likewise unsure of what he indeed might say. And he uttered the first thing that, quite shockingly, came to his mind.

"In Him was life and the life was the light of men."

What! What in the world am I saying? It was as if he was undergoing an out-of-body experience, his mouth opening and voice speaking but the language and vocabulary coming forth was unlike *anything* he had ever spoken.

"I have come that they might have life, and that they might have it more abundantly. And this is eternal life, that they may know You, the only true God, and Jesus Christ whom You have sent." As he spoke these words, the crowd began to buzz, excitedly whispering among themselves.

It was then that Jermaine awoke, but this time his sheets were not sweat soaked, nor was his heart rapidly palpitating in his chest. And equally strange, there were no more feelings of fear gripping his mind as they used to when his dreams ended. Instead, there was a . . . peace. Such an awesome peace that he had never before felt in all his life.

"What's going on?" he whispered, his voice slightly laced with reverential awe. Had . . . had crazy old Ambrose been right about this whole God thing? About his God supposedly revealing unto Jermaine a much greater gift?

But the old man is locked up in a state hospital, remember? Then again, so was he. And did that little fact make him crazy as well? Did jumping off a cliff and attempting to take his own life make him even more crazy?

But what about the greater gift? Jermaine recalled the dream he had just experienced. By no means had he felt terror, fear, or the other emotions typically associated with his recurring nightmare. No, instead he had felt such . . . such an overwhelming joy. And the comforting and loving voice he had heard—had that been real or simply a figment of his own imagination?

Because if it *was* real, then it was, well . . . it was definitely something he wanted.

"Is there a greater gift?" he asked out loud, feeling just a little foolish for doing so. Just who, exactly, was he talking to?

Though no audible voice answered him, deep within his heart, he heard the words as clear and real as if the possessor of the voice were seated next to him on the bed.

"He that hath an ear, let him hear what the Spirit is saying . . . behold I stand at the door and knock. If any man hear my voice, and open the door, I will come into him, and will sup with him and he with me."

As in the dream, Jermaine felt the tingly energy once again begin to engulf his body, filling him with a warmth and love he did not even know existed.

"H-how do I open the door?" Jermaine asked, not knowing that by simply asking such a question, he was in fact preparing his heart to receive the answer.

"And you will seek me and find me, when you search for me with all of Your heart . . ."

And then he knew, in both his spirit and his soul. As he accepted the greater gift of the Lord God breathing life into his very being, this inspirational speaker who had captivated and dazzled audiences all over the country understood for the first time what it truly meant to be . . . *inspired.*

chapter twenty-eight

THE RINGING OF THE phone startled Bell because she didn't receive many calls. Aside from the nurse who came to see her every day, she didn't have that much contact with the outside world.

Picking up the receiver on the fifth ring, she answered with a cautious "Hello?"

"Aunt Bell, this is Jermaine."

She blinked, her mind processing what she thought she had heard. Was her mind messing with her again? The caller had just said his name was . . . his name was . . .

"Did you hear me, Auntie? You remember me, right? Jermaine."

Oh my sweet Jesus . . . "Y-yes, Jermaine. I know's you. Been . . . been long time since I's talked to you last."

"I know. I'm . . . I'm sorry about that, Auntie. I should have been spending some more time with you. I'm . . . I'm sorry about a lot of things."

"S'alright, son. S'alright."

"Yeah. Yeah, well I just wanted you to know something. And I wanted to tell you myself."

"S'alright, son. I's listenin'."

"I . . . I don't know how best to say this, but here it goes. I met Him, Auntie. Jesus." He took a deep breath and made a sound like he was either laughing or crying. Or both. "I met Him . . . and He saved me."

Bell was completely speechless.

"Auntie, did you hear me? The same Jesus you taught me about when I was a kid, but I just wasn't ready to listen. Well, I'm listening now. And He's talking to me."

Warm, wet tears began streaming down her wrinkled face. She felt like—no, she *was* the most blessed person in the world right then. Her reward. Her son. Her promise.

"Thank you, Jesus," she breathed. "Jermaine, I's so . . . I's so happy . . . you's made me so very happy."

• • •

INSTANTLY, JERMAINE'S ENTIRE life began changing in new and exciting ways that caused him to be both happy and hesitant at the same time.

What's happening to me?

He had heard people talk about being *born again*, but he really didn't know what that meant. He couldn't have known what that meant.

Why didn't they tell me it would be like this? As wonderful as this?

He awoke now with a peace and gratitude that he would never have even fathomed existed months ago. It was as if those binding spirits of depression that had ensnared him over ten years ago, shackles that had become a part of his life, had now dropped off and been cast far away from him. He had remembered Aunt Bell reading him passages from the Bible when he was much younger, and how he had thought the old book to be rather boring. Especially with words like *thee* and *thou* and references to things he didn't understand. And as he became older, he started becoming critical and challenged the authenticity of the Bible using the wisdom he thought he had attained from his college education and growing fame.

Now, though, as he began spending countless hours and hours reading the Word, passages in the timeless scriptures seemed to leap out from the pages directly into his heart.

"*But you are a chosen generation, a royal priesthood, a holy nation, His own special people, that you may proclaim the praises of Him who called you out of darkness into His marvelous light.*"

As he re-read and pored over this particular Scripture, a tear sprang from his eye, slid down his cheek, and moistened the page in the Bible.

"Lord, I . . . I didn't know . . . I didn't know," he whispered. He had spent all of his adult life, so-called inspiring people all over the nation with borrowed pet phrases and proven emotional tactics. But the real truth of inspiration was right here before his face. It had always been here, though Jermaine had been unable to see it.

Setting the Bible down on the desk beside him, he dropped to his knees and bowed his head. It was a position that was becoming more and more familiar to him as he communed with the loving Father. Never one to know an earthly father, for the first time Jermaine understood the unconditional, accepting love that a true Father could give. A Father who had always loved him and knew him better than anyone. A Father who could reveal to him what it truly meant to be inspired.

chapter twenty-nine

THE LORD HAS A mighty work for you, Jermaine," Ambrose said as the two sat together in the common meeting area a few weeks later. A Bible lay between them on a chair, opened to the apostle Paul's second epistle to young Timothy.

"What do you mean, a mighty work? Talk like that is still over my head," Jermaine replied with a nervous laugh. "I'm just trying to get to know this Jesus that you . . . well, that you seem to know . . . so well."

Ambrose nodded. "And you will, Jermaine. You will." He gestured to the open Bible in front of him. "But like Paul told Timothy, I remind you to stir up the gift of God that is in you through the laying on of my hands. You have a great gift to reach the masses, Jermaine. God has already given you the blessing of fame, which simply is the platform from which millions of people can listen to what you have to say. You can reach people in a way that not many can. So with the knowledge that God is placing inside you every single day now—I urge you to prepare yourself for that work."

Jermaine nodded thoughtfully. "You know, I used to laugh and ridicule preachers who tried to get everyone to believe what the Bible said. And I wasn't by myself in that thinking, either. Most people thought people like you—"

"Like us," Ambrose gently corrected.

"Like us . . . yeah, like us. People thought we were crazy. I don't know if I'm ready to deal with the drama of that misconception."

Ambrose smiled knowingly before reading the next passage of Scripture from II Timothy. "For God has not given us a spirit of fear, but of power and of love and of a sound mind." He looked up then with steady eyes, which were unwavering and full of faith. "Jermaine, you have nothing to fear, because your testimony will be the thing God uses to fuel that boldness. You remember when I was talking to you about the apostle Paul's conversion?" He pointed to the Bible. "This same man writing to Timothy right here—before his little trip to Damascus, he was the greatest persecutor of Christians the world had ever seen. And after that radical conversion, God gave Him a powerful testimony that put even his harshest critics to shame."

"Yeah, but everyone knows about the life I led. The depression, all those women, the hypocrisy . . ." Jermaine's voice trailed off as he stared down at the floor.

Ambrose placed his hand over Jermaine's. "And that is exactly why your testimony will be even that much more powerful, my son."

• • •

MYRA FINISHED TYPING the last words of the e-mail, then pressed the period key. She whispered a quick, "Thank you, Jesus," as she moved the cursor over the send button. With one click, the e-mail was sent to seventy new distribution outlets for *Song of Solomon* magazine, outlets that would firmly position the magazine as the leader of the urban market share.

"God, you are such a good God," she said aloud.

The ringing of the phone jolted her for a second, but after checking the caller ID, she smiled broadly.

"Xavier, how are you?"

"You know that I am blessed, Myra. You are, too, from what I hear. What's this about getting new subscribers by the hundreds every day?"

"Oh, Xavier, isn't God so, so good! You're hearing right—we've had to expand our subscription department by hiring new customer service reps and drivers. I don't even know how this all happened, especially after what we went through with that whole Jermaine Hill interview, but *Song of Solomon* is selling faster than fried chicken at Uncle Po's family reunion!"

Xavier was silent for a moment. "Who-who's Uncle Po?"

Myra laughed. "Never mind, that wasn't the point. You know, God's blessings toward this magazine and ministry are more than I could have ever asked for. So much more than I could have ever asked for."

"Well then, if it's even possible, I might have some news that might even top that."

"I don't believe that, Xavier. No, not for a second," she replied teasingly. "And besides, I'm not sure that I could even handle more good news. I'm fit to burst right about now, anyway."

"I hope you don't mean that literally, because listen to this: I'm hearing through some very reliable sources that Jermaine Hill has recently accepted Jesus Christ as his personal Lord and Savior."

Myra tried to answer, but her mouth couldn't seem to function just right.

Xavier continued speaking. "He's been at Atascadero, but an old evangelist who's also being treated there has supposedly led him to the Lord."

"S-supposedly?"

"Well, as I said, my source is extremely reliable, but then again, we both know how the media grapevine can get things distorted sometimes."

"Oh, Xavier, but if this . . . if this is true—how awesome that would be! To have one of the most famous celebrities in the nation become saved . . ."

"The effects would be tremendous," Xavier agreed. "I think the most important thing that we need to do—and all of *Song of Solomon*'s prayer team, as well—is to have around-the-clock prayer for Jermaine, that he might be strengthened to be a light and a voice to reach this country in ways not many others could."

"Yes. Yes, you're right." *As you usually are, prayer warrior* . . . "I'll get the word out to our prayer team."

"To God be the glory."

"Amen to that, Xavier. Amen to that."

chapter thirty

TWO WEEKS LATER, Jermaine's early release from Atascadero State Hospital received top billing and exposure from media outlets nationwide. He had become strong enough now to walk out of the hospital without the use of a wheelchair or crutches, albeit moving slowly. The questions posed by everyone from the beat reporters to the prime-time anchors centered on how this once-revered motivational speaker would now integrate himself back into society. On the heels of almost two months of psychiatric treatment, would he dive back into speaking at his usual four to five engagements a week? What was his current mental state? Was he still suicidal? Would the country readily accept him again as one of their beloved icons and heroes?

Mario Jordan had, of course, prepared neatly wrapped press statements to answer all such questions. Seamlessly painting a glorious picture of Jermaine's mental state as being fully recovered and better than ever, he had let it be known with great pride that his client was prepared and ready to once again "get America excited and inspired about life!"

"We did it, J!" Mario now said, excitedly waving a piece of paper over his head like it was worth all the money in the world. The two were in their morning agenda meeting in the executive conference room.

"Did what?" Jermaine asked as he nonchalantly glanced up from the pocket Bible he had begun reading as part of his daily morning devotional. His highly unexpected foray into Christianity naturally had piqued the interest of his agent. At first Mario had feared his star speaker might be turning into a right-wing fundamentalist, but Jermaine had assured him the only thing that had so far changed was his personal relationship with God. And since Jermaine was actually now arriving at his engagements *on time*, and there were no more all-night parties with strange girls, Mario really didn't care about Jermaine's newfound spirituality. As far as Mario was concerned, his client was simply a better, new-and-improved person since his release from the hospital.

"We got ninety-eight percent of the public appeal rating! Once again, we are at the top of the circuit! People better take notes—messin' around with Super Mario will leave you shining his shoes and washing his cars before too long!"

"Your excitement is almost scaring me, Mario. So what if I'm at the top of all the polls? I'm still no higher than the God who gives me the breath to speak."

Mario rolled his eyes as his client *once again* found a way to insert his religious jargon into the conversation. Oh well, at least he wasn't trying to jump off a cliff anymore.

"But J, take a look at these figures—we've got the kind of ratings the networks would kill for."

"That's an interesting way to put it. So I take it you don't mind, then, that I scheduled an interview next week on ABC without running it by you first? I mean, I prayed about it and I just felt it was what the Lord was leading me to do."

Mario rolled his eyes once again. "Well, if you think *God* was leading you to do it, then I guess it's alright, huh?" He couldn't help the small laugh that escaped from his mouth. "Who's doing the interview, by the way? Diane Sawyer? Barbara Walters?"

Jermaine shook his head. "Nope. It's their new girl. A bit ironic, I think, given the circumstances. Chantal Dixon."

Mario gulped and almost choked in the same breath. "W-what? Who did you say?"

"You know, the reporter from *StarWatch News* who first broke the story about me. I'm sure you were aware that ABC hired her, right? Apparently, the network brass thinks it would give the interview an added boost if Chantal conducted it."

"An added boost?" In mere seconds, Mario had grown angry enough to take that pocket Bible of Jermaine's and ram it straight down his client's little golden-voiced throat. "Have you gone *crazy* as well as religious?"

"No, it's like I said earlier. I'm not religious. I just have a relationship with Je—"

"Whatever! The point is still crystal clear—you just signed a death warrant by agreeing to appear on live network television with that crazy woman! She's willing to do whatever she can to take you and me both down. You should have known that by how she had you and that Candace Clark girl followed. For chrissake, Jermaine, you just spent a good two months in a mental hospital because of Chantal Dixon!"

Jermaine calmly eyed Mario. "What was meant for evil has turned out for my good. Spending that time at Atascadero was the best thing that could have happened to me. I was ready—and willing—to kill myself, Mario. Remember? And that had *nothing* to do with Chantal Dixon."

"But ninety-eight percent, Jermaine!" Mario waved the printout of the public opinion poll over his head again. "What would possess you to want to mess up a sure thing? We practically *own* the motivational speaking market, don't you see? Now, one bad interview can flush all that down the toilet!"

Jermaine smiled (with a sense of pity, Mario thought) as he rose to his feet. Tapping his Bible to his heart, he said, "A man's heart plans his way, but the Lord directs his steps."

"Oh, get real! What does that have to do with—"

But the star speaker had turned and was headed out the door. Enraged beyond belief, Mario could barely keep from running after him and beating some common sense back into his twisted, religious little head.

• • •

LATER THAT EVENING, as he casually leaned against the railing on his patio deck, the setting sun gloriously scattering shadows around the lights of Hollywood Hills, Jermaine paused to reflect on the unpredictable twists and turns in his thirty-one years of living.

As had mostly been the case these past few days, his first thoughts were of Aunt Bell. His fond memories of her centered on her stern but loving upbringing of him at a time when there had been nowhere else for him to go. Not only had she been the first person to recognize his natural talent for speaking, but she had also ensured that there were plenty of opportunities for him to exercise that gift in public settings.

"Look into people's eyes when you speak," she had always told him. "And remember that you don't speak jus' 'cause you want to say something. You speak *'cause you have something to say.*" Dutifully and faithfully, she had prayed over him every night before he went to bed until his high school years, anointing his head with oil and pleading for God to direct his path in life. He had rejected that then, dismissing all of it as crazy and religious.

"Oh, but look at God," he thought to himself. *"Look at how God can turn everything around."*

His thoughts then wandered to the good times he had shared with Ronny and Eric. Even now, he would still contend that those two had been taken in the prime of their precious lives—lives that had held such amazing promise and potential. As far as Jermaine was concerned, there was nothing that would've stood in the way of them fulfilling their dreams. Nothing, except of course for that drunk teenage driver with a blood-alcohol level of .65 who had just happened to be speeding down the New Jersey Turnpike in the wrong direction that fateful day almost ten years ago. In his recent days since discovering a relationship with God, Jermaine had repeatedly asked why his two best friends had been tragically taken from him. But there had been no answer from God. Jermaine hadn't known how to embrace such deafening silence other than to accept the reality that sometimes there were no easy answers to life's hard questions.

And then how in the world could he ever free his mind of the wonderful thoughts that were forever kept for Candi Clark?

God, how I miss her . . .

He had never met such an intelligent, poised, and accomplished sistah who was every bit his match and equal in seemingly *every* category. And he was almost certain that he would never meet anyone like her in his life again. She had, to put it plainly, the all-too-rare combination of both brains and beauty that would always leave men reeling in amazement. Jermaine hadn't spoken to her since that awkward, infamous, and now almost-fateful night in the heat of the Phoenix desert several months ago. He had wanted to . . . even had picked up the phone and dialed the first three digits of her number, but he could never follow through. Because what could he possibly say?

"I'm sorry, Candi, for taking advantage of you. And I'm so, so sorry for subjecting you to unthinkable shame and humiliation . . ." Oh yeah, how great was that? Something along those lines would go over just wonderfully.

Still, he remained ever mindful of her description of

her Mr. Right. What had she said again? That she was looking for a man who was unafraid to show emotion in any given circumstances.

I can do that . . .

Someone who was committed to exercising and eating right, and who could make her laugh.

That's me, also . . .

And probably most importantly, someone who believed in God and could grow spiritually with her.

That is definitely, definitely . . . me . . .

But could he in fact be Candi's Mr. Right? After all the unfortunate things that had happened and the horrible mistakes he had made since they had last talked? He still certainly wanted to be. Moreover, the question of whether or not he *could* be such a man did not pain him nearly as much as the thought that he might never get a chance to find out.

chapter thirty-one

THE INTRODUCTORY THEME music to the prime-time show concluded with a resounding flourish. The ominous, solemn bass tones, blended with the short, repetitive trumpet notes, heralded yet another night for this highly rated news program to present the nation with the top insight and analysis of all the current leading stories.

And of course, the network was well aware that there was no story anywhere near as sizzling hot as the Chantal Dixon–Jermaine Hill interview. The live interview tonight was expected to draw more than one hundred million viewers, no less, and why should the demand be anything but extraordinary? In defining duels of epic proportions, most media pundits had raved that it didn't get any better than this. Forget the *Thrilla in Manila*, between Joe Frazier and Muhammad Ali. This was Chantal Dixon grilling Jermaine against the backdrop of the entire nation's watchful eyes. In one corner there was the merciless investigative reporter who had not only scooped the secret relationship with Candace Clark but who had also provided the exclusive and incriminating report of Jermaine's suicidal tendencies. And in the other corner sat the country's foremost motivational speaker who had just undergone two months of treatment in a state hospital, now publicly declaring he was fully recovered, healed, and ready to resume his speaking career.

In the master control room, veteran news director Tim Kasdan watched the two rows of five television monitors like a famished hawk studying a tasty mouse scurrying about in an open field. His right-hand man, the technical director, listened attentively for the instructions on which camera shot to take.

"Stand by camera two," Tim said.

On the set, Chantal Dixon flashed her now instantly recognizable smile to the national audience that awaited her. She sat tall and confident in the oversize armchair, which not by accident but by choosing was the same chair used by Barbara Walters when she had conducted the famous interview of Monica Lewinsky years ago. And because appearance spoke volumes in these types of settings, Chantal had chosen to dress in a conservative navy business suit, lightly accented with subdued makeup and accessories to convey the no-nonsense image that worked so well for her.

Directly across from her, and opposite in appearance, sat a seemingly relaxed Jermaine Hill clad in a casual beige- and cream-colored suit. His long legs were leisurely crossed at the knees and the smile he wore matched Chantal's. Like her, he was the picture of confidence and readiness.

"Roll tape!" Tim commanded, a throwback term from the days when television studios had, in fact, used tape. Of course, the technology was all digital now but Tim still loved to employ those old Cronkite-era terms. At any rate, his crew knew what he meant, and that was all that mattered.

"Tape rolling!"

"Take camera two!"

As the theme music faded, the microphones were cued up and on the set, the floor director gave the hand signal for Chantal to begin.

"Good evening. Today is Friday, November tenth, and we welcome you to this edition of *Eye on America*. My name is Chantal Dixon and tonight I am joined in the studio by a man who has been no stranger recently to controversy and scandal." She paused a bit, her facial expression a cross between a smile and a smirk. Then she shifted slightly in her seat to face another camera.

"Take camera three," Tim voiced back in the master control room.

Chantal continued reading from the teleprompter script inside the face of camera three. "Jermaine Hill is widely considered to be the foremost motivational speaker in the country, with revenues from the sales of his tapes and attendance at his popular seminars reaching numbers of unprecedented proportions. However, in early July of this year, a story was released alleging that the public image and persona of this charismatic inspirational speaker might in fact be radically at odds with a private life dominated by severe depression and secretive playboy trysts that would cause even Hugh Hefner to raise his eyebrows.

"And then came the spectacular suicide attempt captured by television cameras all over the nation. Jermaine Hill leaped off Hollywood's Mount Lee, seeking to take his own life in dramatic fashion. The unsuccessful attempt landed him first in the hospital for serious injuries and then under the probe of an investigation into the life and affairs of this seemingly perfect inspirational speaker. Now, after spending ten weeks undergoing psychiatric treatment in California's Atascadero State Hospital, Mr. Hill is back yet again in the public eye, touring across the country and giving inspirational seminars. But has he *truly* recovered from his clinical depression? And is he now fit to once again be regarded as the premier expert on inspiration and motivation? These questions and others will be addressed in a live interview with Jermaine Hill and yours truly right after these words from our sponsors. Stay tuned, America."

• • •

RESTING IN HER living room, Candace set the remote control down on the coffee table and proceeded to comfortably stretch out on her sofa. Like most everyone else in the country, she was attentively watching the interview, and doing so with a multitude of mixed feelings.

She had not seen or spoken to Jermaine since that night in Scottsdale, and so much had passed through her mind about him—what had really caused him to feel so depressed as to attempt suicide, how his treatments had gone at the mental hospital, how he was doing now, and so on—questions that probably would never be answered for her. Such a possibility saddened her; because despite all the negative and damaging publicity she had received as a result of his actions, she still treasured her brief time with him and held a soft spot in her heart for him.

She knew it didn't make any sense at all. Her own reputation had in all likelihood been forever scarred because of this man, yet why did she often find herself still fondly thinking about him? She even found herself taking the time to pray about him—asking her heavenly Father to watch over and protect him. And that's what she began doing at that moment, uttering a short prayer that Jermaine would fare alright during this interview. For she thought it more than a little strange that he had even agreed to go on live with somebody like Chantal Dixon. It was no secret that the woman harbored a personal grudge against the man with the golden voice.

• • •

"WELCOME BACK, everyone, to *Eye on America*. I am now joined live here in the studio with Jermaine Hill."

"Take camera one," Tim said in the control room, giving the viewers at home the chance to see both Chantal and Jermaine in the same wide-angle shot.

"Jermaine, it's good to have you with us here tonight," Chantal began.

"Thank you."

"I have to begin with the question I'm sure is on everyone's mind. Just what were you thinking when you decided to do a televised jump off of Mount Lee?"

Jermaine shrugged ever so slightly. "First of all, I hadn't planned for it to be televised, Chantal. Interesting how *that* came about, isn't it? Anyway, I suppose it was a culmination of things, really. There was a lot in my life that I wasn't happy with and wasn't dealing properly with. I had been thinking about committing suicide for a good while, and that night I . . . I guess I thought I was finally ready to go through with it."

"You said there were many things in your life that you weren't happy with. Yet while all this had been going on, you were still continually before the public, exciting and inspiring them about life. Do you not feel that you were being a bit hypocritical?"

"When I was out there speaking, in many ways it was just a performance. I could consciously detach the person I was from the job I was doing."

"So you do, then, agree that you were leading a hypocritical lifestyle?" Chantal was going in for the kill.

"Yes."

"And how has anything changed? Are you saying that merely ten weeks of psychiatric treatment were sufficient to completely heal you of depression and your suicidal tendencies? Do you expect the American public to believe that you are no longer giving motivational speeches as simply *performances*?"

"Yes, Chantal, in fact there has been quite a big change. However, I also know that hospitalization for ten weeks is not enough to effectively cure me of the issues I was suffering with, and I am not crediting doctors and psychiatrists alone with the success of my recovery."

"Wait a minute, I'm not quite understanding you.

You have been quoted as saying that you are fully recovered and healed from clinical depression. Yet you just stated that the doctors at the state hospital were not fully responsible for such a recovery. To whom, then, are you crediting your healing?"

Perhaps if Chantal had not been so bent on prosecuting Jermaine as though the two of them were in a court of law and she was judge, jury, and executioner, then she might have realized that she was being masterfully set up.

"I fully credit my healing and renewed gift to inspire people about life to none other than . . . Jesus Christ."

Five to ten seconds passed before Chantal realized her jaw had unprofessionally dropped open. In her earpiece, the show's producer was screaming at her to come back to reality. They *were* on live television, after all.

"I-I'm sorry," she stammered. "D-did I hear you right? You are crediting your recovery to . . . to . . ."

Jermaine smiled. "Yes, that is right. To none other than Jesus Christ. I'm fully aware that speaking His name on live network television is not the politically correct thing to do, but frankly I don't care."

For the first time ever while in front of a camera, Chantal Dixon was completely and utterly . . . *speechless.*

Jermaine took the liberty to continue. "You see, I've had to learn the hard way that fame and riches certainly don't guarantee you a happy life, I don't care who you are. Because though I was motivating millions of people, I honestly didn't have a clue about what it truly meant to be excited and inspired about life. It took an encounter with Almighty God to reveal unto me what inspiration truly meant."

The producer was now in the throes of a hysterical fit, pleading with Chantal through her earpiece to interrupt Jermaine's whole religious spiel by announcing that they would be going to a commercial break. But Chantal could only sit there, dumbfounded. It seemed almost as if some unseen force was preventing her from interrupting Jermaine as he spoke.

So he was free and uninhibited for the next few minutes to give his testimony of salvation, redemption, and true inspiration to a record-setting television audience, a miracle of unparalleled proportions that only God Himself could receive glory out of.

chapter thirty-two

THE REACTION AND fallout from Jermaine's stirring testimony on *Eye on America* was swift and immediate, dominating radio talk shows and newspaper headlines in the following days from the Big Apple to Hollywood and everywhere in between. Church leaders from various Christian denominations praised the boldness of their newest "soldier in the Lord's army." Fellow speakers along the motivational circuit cautioned that Jermaine's newfound religious fervor might affect his agenda when speaking. Even the president of the United States issued a brief statement, declaring that Americans everywhere should be proud of their constitutional right to freedom of religion, and the free exercise thereof. It seemed that everyone had an opinion to share concerning this American idol's radical conversion to Christianity—everyone including an irate and agitated Mario Jordan, who was forced to immediately attempt to put a liberal spin on his client's words.

"Jermaine, there goes the ninety-eight percent of the public's approval rating," he dourly relayed over the phone to his client, who was at the moment en route from Chicago to Los Angeles. "And with that in mind, some sponsors are no doubt going to be pulling their endorsements of you. I hope you realize how massive and far-reaching a mistake you may have made."

Presently flying somewhere over the Great Plains, Jermaine rolled his eyes in the first-class seat of his chartered plane. "Mario, for the last time, everything is *not* always about money and sponsorships."

"He-llllooo! Earth to Jermaine! What, am I next going to hear on the news that you're giving to the poor and needy? This is a *money-making* business, J. And as your agent, I—"

"As my agent, your first priority is to respect the wishes of your client," Jermaine cut in. "And as far as what I said last week on TV, it doesn't matter one way or the other what happens. I can handle the consequences."

Mario sighed loudly, with exasperation. "J, tell me this. How does this change us? I mean, we've built an entire empire on the whole golden-voice shtick. What we have going for us works, man. Are you telling me that you're now turning into some kind of Billy Graham / T. D. Jakes wannabe?"

Jermaine let out a short laugh. "No, Mario. I'm still all about getting people excited and inspired about life. Even more so, I'd say now. Sure, my relationship with God is going to change my life in some ways—but only for the better. My faith is going to make me a more effective speaker, because now this won't be just a performance. I'm truly going to want to see people's lives changed. Look, I'll talk to you in a couple of days when I get back to L.A."

"A couple of days? What are you talking about? I scheduled some last-minute appearances for you tonight and tomorrow at the Convention Center."

"No-can-do, Mario. Besides, haven't I told you not to do that last-minute scheduling without checking with me first?"

"Yeah, I know, but J, the money was too good to pass up."

"Sorry, Mario, but I've got plans elsewhere."

"J! Okay, wait, wait. Where are you going, though? I should know of any changes to your itinerary, you know."

"There's something I need to take care of in Houston, my man. Talk to you later." With a huge smile on his face, he hung up the phone before his agent could say more.

• • •

FOR SOME REASON, Candace was having the hardest time concentrating as she stared at the blank sheet of paper in front of her. A week earlier, she had gladly accepted an offer to write a feature for the M. D. Anderson hospital system highlighting the latest breakthroughs in cancer research. Though she had been given more than enough information, she thus far had been unable to organize the thick, three-inch binder of medical research into anything remotely resembling a readable feature article. She knew why, of course. Her mind was still crazily turning cartwheels over Jermaine's testimony on *Eye on America* last week. How awesome had that been—to see a man of such stature and standing in the public eye share his newfound faith in the Lord Jesus Christ!

Almost like an answer to my prayers . . .

And that poor little Chantal Dixon—Candace knew that such a catastrophic blunder committed while conducting an interview of that importance would probably demote that girl to doing weekend fashion reports or something. The networks didn't play when it came to unforgivable mistakes like that.

The ringing chime of the doorbell interrupted her unproductivity and, glad for an excuse to break away for a moment, she got up and padded in her stockinged feet to the front door. Not even thinking to look through the peephole because she had already figured that it was probably her always-vacationing neighbor asking yet again for Candace to collect her mail, she opened the door . . .

. . . and in the same second that her mouth fell open, her heart started beating faster and the heat she felt had absolutely *nothing* to do with the warm, muggy temperature of the Bayou City.

chapter thirty-three

SHE WAS . . . BEAUTIFUL . . . so, so beautiful in Jermaine's eyes. And not the kind of unrealistic, super-model, magazine cover-girl beauty that once exclusively served to stir his attractions. No, the beauty that Candi Clark possessed radiated from the inside out, permeating every aspect of her being so that he was sure if he gazed long enough he would behold an angelic glow framing her body.

For a good while, neither spoke. Their eyes were locked into each other with a long-lost sense of reunion and of knowing: theirs were two lives linked together beyond the controversy and scandal that had gone before.

"Candi, I'm sorry," he finally whispered, his voice barely audible.

She nodded.

He cleared his throat and continued. "I mean, I know those two words aren't enough to atone for all the hurt and pain I must have caused you, but—"

"Shh . . ." she gently interrupted. "I accept your apology, Jermaine. But I do have to say, it is *long* past due."

He sheepishly grinned. “Well, I’ve been unavoidably preoccupied, I guess you could say. I didn’t have an opportunity to contact you.”

She gave him a doubting look. “Jermaine, please. You’ve been out of the crazy house for almost a full month now.”

“Hey! It wasn’t a crazy—”

“Just kidding,” she said smoothly. “Now come on in, before somebody sees you out here and calls the *National Enquirer.*”

• • •

“THE PRESS WAS that bad, huh?” Jermaine asked as he took a seat on the sofa in Candace’s sunroom.

“Worse than bad. Capital A aa-awful! No disrespect to her memory, but I felt like Princess Diana with all the paparazzi keeping me locked in here like a prisoner. They couldn’t set foot on my lawn, but they could legally camp out all along the street. And for about a week, that’s what they did. And after everything sort of died down, I would still notice a couple of reporters following me around the city.”

“They’re still doing that?”

She shrugged. “Every once in a while I’ll still spot one. It’s not that bad, I suppose. Probably nothing like what *you* have to go through, I’m sure.” She collected the two glasses of sparkling cider from the bar and walked over to the sofa, handing one to Jermaine.

“Thank you.” He held up the glass. “What are we celebrating?”

“How about . . . a new life in Christ?” she asked, her face instantly brightening with the suggestion.

"A definite cause for celebration," Jermaine agreed as they clinked their glasses.

"Jermaine, what you did on *Eye on America* last week, well . . . I thought it was so inspiring, and so—"

"It had *nothing* to do with me, Candi. Honestly. I definitely didn't plan to say what I did . . . it just kind of came out. I mean, I'm new to this whole Christian lifestyle, y'know? And being in the public eye so much, I know that people are constantly watching me, waiting to see if I'm going to slip up. I just want to be real about all this."

Candace offered an encouraging nod. "My advice to you would be to find a good church home out there in L.A. and make sure to have some accountability people in your life."

"People like Mario?" he asked. They both laughed.

"No, definitely *not* people like Mario. You need to be praying for that brotha. He may be keeping your bank accounts and speaking schedule full, but what you really need are people that truly care about you and want to see you develop and mature as a Christian man."

"People, then, like . . . like *you*?" He studied her face closely, noticing with great interest the definite pause she took before answering the somewhat personal question.

"Yes, Jermaine," she replied, blushing slightly. "Of course I want to . . . um, well, I would still like to be a part of your life."

He set his half-empty glass on a coaster on the table. "You know, Candi, about that walk on Venice Beach, and then that night in the hotel room in Phoenix, what

I did—how I acted toward you—I'd like to think those were the actions of the old Jermaine." He rubbed his chin for a moment. "Physical intimacy was the only way I knew how to show you I really cared for you. I didn't mean to cross the line with you and make you feel . . . uncomfortable in any way."

He looked up then, gazing fully into her brown eyes. "If you give me another chance, I'd like to try to find new ways to show you that I . . . that I still care for you."

"Jermaine . . ." She, too, set her glass on the table and rubbed her hands together. "Jermaine, so much has happened between the both of us. I . . . I don't know what to say. I . . . I just don't know . . ."

No! No! I am not about to lose you again . . .

"Candi, I came here not just to apologize for what I put you through, but also to tell you that for the life of me, I cannot stop thinking about you. I can't get you out of my mind and I don't want to, either. Spending that time with you and getting to know you was . . ." He started rubbing his chin again.

"Was what?" she asked, leaning forward a little on the couch.

"Well, let me just say that I never . . . *never* wanted your interview to end. I loved spending my days with you, trying to . . . trying to keep you from seeing the *real* me. But then I guess all my efforts really didn't matter, huh? I mean there's nothing like jumping off a cliff to bring out the worst in a guy."

"Jermaine, for what it's worth, I never saw you as someone without hope. Everybody has problems. At the time, you just hadn't found the real answer to those problems. But I think you have, now."

"I *know* I have, Candi. Finding Jesus was the best thing that could have ever happened to me." He cocked his head ever so slightly, never losing his eye contact with her. "And just maybe, the second-best thing that could happen to me is showing you that I'm your Mr. Right."

"Jermaine, I . . . I . . ."

"No, hear me out, alright? You were looking for a man who's sensitive and open about displaying his emotions, hmm?" Instantly, he made a pitifully sad face, sniffling and pretending he was crying. Moments later, an actual tear fell from the corner of his right eye. "See? I can even cry on command. Take that, Oprah!"

Candace started laughing.

"And you were looking for a man committed to eating right and exercising? Well, Mario's got me on this diet and taking sessions with a personal trainer four times a week. I mean, this guy's like Rambo or something." He flexed his muscles and in an Arnold Schwarzenegger–type voice, proclaimed, "I vont to . . . pump you up!"

More laughter from Candace.

"Let's see, what else. You wanted a man who believed in God and could grow spiritually with you, right? Candi, you know I'm a believer now and nothing would make me happier than growing in Christ with you. So you see, I could be your Mr. Right."

By now, Candace had to dab her eyes to keep tears of laughter from streaking down her face. "But you . . . you forgot something," she wheezed, finally calming herself. "You forgot . . . that I was also looking for a man who could make me laugh."

Jermaine gave Candace exactly two seconds before he plucked a pillow from the sofa and playfully threw it at her. And he had even less time before she, still laughing, sent it right back at him.

chapter thirty-four

THE INSIDE OF the sanctuary was precisely as Jermaine remembered. He hadn't set foot inside these antiquated walls in years, but even after all this time the decorative and structural uniformity was not surprising. Calvary Church of Holiness had been established over a century ago upon the types of religious tenets not especially given to change.

His fingers now lingered on the back of each pew as he made his way down the center aisle. This place held more memories of his childhood than anywhere else.

"You sit your behind down right there and don't you move," his Aunt Bell had scolded him every Sunday.

"Poor Aunt Bell," he thought, smiling. He had never learned to stay still on those hard, wooden seats.

A door toward the rear of the church opened then and a partly stooped-over elderly man emerged.

"Mercy alive! If it ain't Bell's little man all growed up!" bellowed Deacon Parker.

"I'm not so little anymore," Jermaine responded as he shook the outstretched hand of the old deacon. The man looked exactly as he had the last time Jermaine had seen him.

"I see that, sho' I do." The two held hands for a while, simply looking at each other. "How's Bell?" the deacon asked.

"Doing about the same. She has her bad days mixed with good days, but I think she's ready to . . . you know . . . ready to . . ."

"Sho' she's ready. Bell's been ready to go home and be with the Lord jus' about all her life. Yessah, I sho' believe that." With that, the deacon shuffled over to the wall and flipped on three switches. In seconds, the overhead lighting throughout the building flickered on.

"I see you're still opening everything up on Sunday mornings," Jermaine observed. "You've been doing that a long time."

"Over sixty years," the deacon responded with a wide grin. "But this mornin', I's specially proud to open the Lord's house. A special preacher be in our midst today."

Jermaine was going to ask to whom he was referring before realizing that special preacher was none other than himself.

• • •

"I NEVER IMAGINED I'd be one day standing in this pulpit," Jermaine began speaking. Every room was filled to capacity as this church welcomed one of their own back in grand fashion.

"All my life, I've heard about my family's spiritual

heritage but it has never meant so much to me as it does today. My Aunt Bell . . . oh, God. I owe so much . . . to the prayers and strength of Bell Davis."

"Amen!" a woman seated on the front pew shouted, prompting loud applause throughout the sanctuary.

"I didn't realize how great a sacrifice it was to take me and raise me like she did," Jermaine continued. "I know she couldn't be here today, but I want all of you to know how much I love her. I wouldn't be alive before you today if not for her daily prayers over my life. I tell her that every day now and I hope in some small way she will know how thankful I am."

He paused to step back from the podium. Many in the congregation today had known him when he was a child. They undoubtedly had countless stories to share about him, and because of that, they were still family—for better or worse.

"I want to give you a preview of the new Jermaine Hill," he said. "Most of you have followed my career since I left Baltimore, and there have been great moments, bad moments, and everything else in between. But through all of that, I've somehow been tagged as the one person who can get you excited and inspired about life."

He was glad Mario wasn't present to try and spin his next words.

"The public had it all wrong. As everyone knows, I couldn't even get *myself* excited about life. I learned the hard way that there's only One who can. There's only One who is worthy of all the attention and praise. His name is Jesus."

The same woman loudly shouted, "Amen!"

"Over the past months, I've had time to ponder over the key issues in my life. Many times, I've asked myself why God blessed me with a gift to speak. I mean, why me?"

He pointed to a spot on the floor just to his left. "I can remember standing right there as a child, reciting an Easter speech and loving every minute of it."

"I was there!" the woman shouted. "I remember that. You was good, too!"

Jermaine smiled at her. "Thank you. I knew then that I was meant to be a speaker. I don't know why God also allowed my name to become famous. Sometimes, that is just as much of a curse as it is a blessing. But I *do* know one thing—I'm now committed to using that same fame to spread the message of God's love throughout the land. These messages you will hear me speaking now will be the most inspiring, empowering words I've ever spoken, and the ears of the nation will be listening.

"So are you ready to go to the next level in your life? Are you ready to have everything God intended for you?"

He smiled then, because *some* things just never changed.

"Well, let Jermaine give you some simple suggestions . . ."

epilogue

One year later, Christmas Day

THE PRIVATE, SECLUDED ceremony was intimate and invitation-only, with good reason. For the past few months, rumors had been running rampant that Jermaine Hill was to wed Candace Clark, though it was anyone's guess as to where and when such a high-profile event would take place.

The two celebrities had both realized it was crazy for them to continue secretly seeing each other like their relationship was some kind of illicit affair. Either he would fly in to Houston for a few days when his speaking schedule would allow, or she would invent some last-minute reason to go to Los Angeles. They were fooling nobody, and it was simply a matter of time before the whole country would know it. So they had decided to stop hiding their intentions.

On New Year's Eve of that year, they had arrived, hand-in-hand at the Times Square celebration in New York City. Their appearance together was such a surprise that even the normally unflappable Dick Clark was momentarily at a loss for words on live television. Nobody, but nobody, could ever remember *that* happening before. And the couple's anticipated midnight kiss completely overshadowed the countdown. After everyone got down to five, four, three . . . all eyes were on Candace and Jermaine. Forget about the ball dropping . . .

"It's Official! They're a Couple!" screamed the headlines of every paper the following day, a feat that in itself threatened to upstage the New Year's Day parade coverage. It seemed like the nation couldn't get enough of celebrity dating, and at the moment there was no relationship bigger than this motivational speaker and the celebrated writer. They were besieged with requests to do shows together—*Live with Regis, Oprah, The Tonight Show*, but they chose to grant an interview to only one media source—Myra Washington. As a result, *Song of Solomon*'s readership grew in record numbers to surpass all competitors and become the leading urban interest magazine in America. So much had happened in the past year . . . but the biggest occasion of all was yet to happen.

• • •

AMBROSE RIVERS nodded, as if to give the signal, at the seated congregants in the small chapel located on a tiny island off the Jamaican coast. Fully released from Atascadero six months ago, he now traveled full-time with Jermaine as the speaker's personal spiritual advisor.

"Dearly beloved, we are gathered here together to celebrate this blessed union of holy matrimony between Candace Clark and Jermaine Hill." He paused to look closely at the bride and the groom. "God is good, is he not? And what He has joined together, let no man put asunder . . ."

He continued to recite scriptures pertaining to love and marriage, but for the moment Jermaine did not hear them. As a matter of fact, he was hearing nothing—everything was so still, so quiet. So beautiful. He could only focus on the beautiful lady standing directly in front of him. It was hard to believe that he had known her for only a year and a half. He felt like he had known her all of his life.

"Jermaine, I believe you have have chosen to perform your own vows . . ."

He thought someone was speaking to him as he stood there, mesmerized by his future wife.

"Jermaine?"

He rubbed his chin. "Y-yes. Yes. Candi, I have waited my whole life to share my love with a woman so special, so . . . precious. And I'm so thankful to God, because you have been worth every second of that wait. I promise to love you, Candi, with all that is in my heart. I will cherish and honor you as the royal queen that you are. You are my inspiration, my world, my earth. For better or worse, I will be right here supporting and loving you. I am honored to call you mine. And I am more honored . . . to be called *yours*."

Ambrose turned to the bride. "Candace?"

She nodded in understanding as the tears began

rolling down her face. She needed a few moments to regain her composure.

"Jermaine. Because I'm standing here with you, this . . . this is the happiest day of my life. All that has happened to the both of us has only caused my love for you to grow stronger. I promise to stand with you through good times and bad. And whether we're up or down—know that my love for you will remain constant and true."

She smiled fully at him and it took every ounce of his restraint not to lift the veil from her face and take her in his arms right there.

"Jermaine," she continued, "I love you as a man that follows after God's heart. I love you as a man who reaches and touches the lives of so many people. You . . . *are* my Mr. Right! And I love you . . . as a man inspired."

Her last words melted him as they found their way right into the depths of his heart. *"Inspired,"* he thought to himself. *"I am, aren't I? This . . . this is what living is all about . . ."*

reading group guide

Prologue

In his journey to fame and fortune, Jermaine had "discovered that the only person he could really trust was himself, which in turn became a problem once he began to forget just who he himself was." Do you see a certain irony in the contrast between Jermaine and his Aunt Bell, caught in the fog of Alzheimer's disease? How is the source of their trust (and therefore, their hope) different? (See Proverbs 3:5–6.) In whom do you place *your* trust?

Chapter I

Candace had one room in her home that was a sanctuary, a place where she did no work, a refuge from the world, "where she could fully celebrate being a woman—and where she could taste the savory fruits of success." Everyone needs a space for sanctuary—in effect, a Sabbath space. God established the Sabbath, a day of rest, when he himself rested after creating the world (Genesis 2:1–2). Where and when in your life have you created such a Sabbath—in time *and* in space?

Chapter 2

The friendship Jermaine had had with Eric and Ronny had been incredibly precious and rare, especially among men. Do you have that kind of relationship with anyone in your life—past or present? With whom? What makes that friendship so valuable? Scripture describes two such friendships: in I Samuel 20 and in the book of Ruth. (Also see Proverbs 17:17; 27:6,17; Ecclesiastes 4:7–12; John 15:12–13.)

Chapter 3

Publishing *Song of Solomon* was a dream come true for Myra, a dream she had birthed two decades earlier while still in college. What's your dream? How long have you been harboring it? What steps, if any, have you taken to make it come true? Share your dream—and write it down (Habakkuk 2:2–3). And, as God leads, plot out the next steps in bringing that vision to pass.

Chapter 4

What do you think of Ambrose at this point in the story? Is he a prophet? a fanatic? socially or criminally insane? He thinks of himself as a modern-day John the Baptist. Check out Luke 3:1–20 and do your own comparison study.

Chapter 5

Jemiaine views Mario's expressions of concern as being motivated more by business than personal reasons. What do you think? Do you have people in your life like Mario—whose motives in the relationship are suspect? How do you interact with them? What does Scripture advise in such situations? (See Proverbs 19:4,6; 20:6; Matthew 7:6, 15–20; 10:16.)

Chapter 6

"It's not a good idea to start a relationship with a guy you practically keep on a pedestal. . . . So when Prince Charming turns out to be less than perfect, you're staring at a serious wake-up call," Candi warns Tasha. Do you agree or disagree? Why? How can we approach our relationships realistically while still leaving room for the romance?

Chapter 7

Jermaine knew that his image, his message, his whole life was a mirage . . . an illusion. He was the premiere motivational speaker in the country, and he had difficulty motivating himself to get up each day. In fact, he was seriously and creatively contemplating suicide. He knew himself to be a fraud, but he continued the performance. Why? Why do any of us daily don our masks, even recognizing them for what they are? What keeps us from being real—and asking for the help we desperately need (Proverbs 14:12)?

Chapter 8

A question-and-answer game . . . Ambrose poised himself for it in his session with his psychologist. Candace and Jermaine positioned themselves for it in their initial meeting. We do it in job interviews, on first dates, and in small talk at social gatherings. How do you engage in such "games"? How does your position going into the game determine what you get out of it? (Scripture records a variety of occasions when Jesus engaged at different levels in the game. See Mark 2:18–3:6; 10:17–27; 11:27–33; 12:13–37.)

Chapter 9

Candace always opened an interview with the same two questions because she knew they caught people off guard—and revealed a lot about them. Answer those two questions yourself: What is your favorite book (and why)? What is the last book you read, and why did you choose it?

Chapter 10

Aunt Bell continues to intercede tirelessly for Jermaine, claiming the scriptural promise in Proverbs 22:6. What does that Scripture mean to you—as the child of your own parents or guardian and as a parent (or parent figure) to other children? How have you experienced its fulfillment?

Chapter 11

What would it look like for you to find someone with whom you "connect on every level"? (See Genesis 2:18–25.) Is that person out there—or have you already found him? Do you believe in love at first sight, soul mates, that sort of thing? Why or why not?

Chapter 12

Jermaine shared his "most embarrassing moment" story, identifying the lesson he learned from the experience: "Sometimes it's better to be heard and not seen." Do you agree or disagree? Why? In what situations is it better to be heard? In what situations might being seen be better?

Chapter 13

Unbeknownst to Jermaine, while he was wrestling with depression and suicidal thoughts on the inside, Chantal and Spike were plotting an attack from the outside. Have you ever had days, weeks, months—even years like that—when you feel embattled from within and without? Have you ever felt the struggle of life and death within your own spirit? Paul did. Read 2 Corinthians 4:7–18 for his response to such feelings.

Chapter 14

Candace tells Jermaine that getting married is the highlight of every woman's life. Do you agree or disagree? Why? If you disagree, what do you think is (or should be) the highlight? Then, Jermaine tells Candi that the secret to winning any woman's heart is the ability to make her laugh. Agree or disagree? Why? What's the secret to winning your heart?

Chapter 15

Jermaine was adamant about declining the latest lucrative guest appearance—because it interfered with his plans to be with Candi. Do you think he was learning that money isn't everything? Why or why not? (See Proverbs 23:4–5; Matthew 6:24; and 1 Timothy 6:6–10, 17–19 for scriptural insights about wealth.)

Chapter 16

Ask yourself Jermaine's motivational question, "What *is* the big time, exactly?" In other words, how do you define success? How does God define it? See Proverbs 3:1–18; Matthew 5:1–12; Luke 12:13–21; and 1 Corinthians 13.

Chapter 17

Jermaine and Candi almost make love together—but she finally calls a halt. Why? Did she do the right thing? Why or why not? If so, did she do it for the right reasons?

Chapter 18

Jermaine is absolutely devastated by what he interprets as Candace's rejection. It seems to underscore every other rejection or abandonment he has suffered in life. When you are feeling abandoned, rejected, and alone, where do you go and to whom do you turn? Consider opening your Bible to these passages: Psalm 40, 42, 46, 121, 130; Romans 8:26–28.

Chapter 19

Myra had staked her dream on this feature interview between Candace and Jermaine—now it appeared that the golden opportunity had turned to lead. Even as Xavier prayed, Myra's mind raced with worries, plans, and strong emotions. When have you faced a comparable situation? How did you respond? How would Scripture advise us? (See Psalm 46 and John 14:27.)

Chapter 20

How did the abrupt swarm of paparazzi serve as an answer to Aunt Bell's prayer? When has an apparently negative incident in your life proved to be your salvation in the long run?

Chapter 21

The relationship between Jennaine's suicidal urges and his sanity has been questioned repeatedly throughout the story. Now that he has actually made an attempt on his life, the question is finally called: What do you think? Is Jermaine crazy? Explain.

Chapter 22

In the aftermath of Jermaine's suicide attempt and the tabloid exposé, Myra was dealing with "an epic faith-crisis," in God and in herself. Xavier counseled her to take heart that "sometimes God allows trying situations to best His children only so their faith might be strengthened and established." Paul offers much the same reassurance in Romans 5:3–5; so does James in James 1:2–4. How have you experienced the harvest of good fruit from trying times?

Chapter 23

Ambrose tells Jermaine that listening and hearing are two quite different things. What's the difference? How does James's exhortation in James 1:22–25 illustrate the principle Ambrose is hinting at?

Chapter 24

Jermaine is tormented by a recurring dream. It is powerful and terrifying to him. You can guess that it has spiritual significance in his life. What do you think it means? Have you ever had a recurring dream of that caliber, one that you suspect is God trying to get your attention? How do you respond to such dreams?

Chapter 25

Jermaine once declared the secret to happiness and success is to "do what you love and love what you do." Ambrose now observes that "what you *do*, is not who you *are.*" If you really love what you do, however, it is easy to start equating that doing with your being. We do it casually when we answer the question "Who are you?" with a relational or vocational response, instead of with our name (e.g., "I'm Ryan's mom" or "I'm a freelance writer and editor"). How do you balance the two truisms in your own life—both in your relationships (*whom* you love) and in your vocation *(what* you love)?

Chapter 26

For Candace, returning to church was like coming home. Have you ever experienced that feeling—the unconditional love and willing forgiveness of the Holy Spirit—even just the warm embrace of sisters and brothers in Christ after an absence from your home congregation? Read Jesus' parable about the prodigal (in Luke 15:11–32) through Candi's eyes—and walking that long road home yourself in the prodigal's shoes.

Chapter 27

Jermaine is finally beginning to understand his dream—and the suffocating sensation of being unable to breathe. He is making the connection between the etymological meaning of the word *inspire* and the word *breath.* They are the same (e.g., *respiratory* disease refers to breathing disorders). How have you experienced the relationship between the two—inspiration and breath? Check out the familiar story in Ezekiel 37 for a powerful illustration of the connection among breath, spirit, life, and inspiration.

Chapter 28

Jermaine's call to Aunt Bell with news of his saving encounter with Jesus was balm to her soul. How do you think his confession of faith to the woman who raised him affected Jermaine? Talk about the power of your testimony—to those who hear it (saved and unsaved) and to you yourself. What does Scripture say about that dynamic? (See Romans 1:16–17; 10:9–10; Revelation 12:10–12.)

Chapter 29

Ambrose cites 2 Timothy 1:6–7 as he disciples Jermaine in a discovery of God's call on his life. What gifts are hidden in you, placed there by the laying on of hands (or any other inspired impartation)? How can you stir them up and use them for God? (Read also 2 Timothy 3:14–4:5.)

Chapter 30

Jermaine told Mario he wasn't religious. He just had a relationship with Jesus. What's the difference? How does a relationship with Christ change us in a way that religion doesn't? How has his new faith changed Jermaine?

Chapter 31

How did Jermaine's interview with Chantal powerfully (and humorously!) illustrate the truth in Paul's assurance in Romans 8:26–27? How have you experienced such mediation and intercession on your behalf on the part of the Holy Spirit?

Chapter 32

Did Jermaine's decision to remain on the motivational-speaking circuit surprise you? Why or why not? Sometimes, in the church, we assume a person with a gift for speaking and inspiring people should go into church or parachurch ministry—as Mario put it, in the style of Billy Graham or T. D. Jakes. Should our most gifted speakers all end up behind a pulpit of some kind? Why or why not? (Read Romans 12:3–8; Ephesians 4:7,11–13.)

Chapter 33

Candi encouraged Jermaine to find a good home church and people to hold him accountable and disciple him in his growth and maturity as a Christian man. Do you have a faith community and people in your life who can do that for you? Why or why not? If you are going through these questions in a small group, how can the members be that for one another—giving and receiving?

Epilogue

Jermaine and Candace had discovered in each other their own Ms. and Mr. Right. And, at their wedding they spoke vows they had written themselves. If you find Mr. Right, what original vows will you speak on your future wedding day? What is it you are willing to promise?